ON THE ROPE

G000019914

ABOUT THE AUTHOR

Erich Hackl, born in Steyr, Austria, studied German and
Spanish and worked as a teacher and editor for several
years. He now works in Madrid and Vienna as a writer
and translator. Based on true events, his books include
Aurora's Motive and *Farewell Sidonia*, which feature on
school curricula. Hackl has received numerous awards.

ON THE ROPE

A Hero's Story

ERICH HACKL

Translated by Stephen Brown

Published in 2020 by
Haus Publishing Ltd
4 Cinnamon Row
London SW11 3TW
www.hauspublishing.com

Originally published under the title *Am Seil*

Copyright © 2018 by Diogenes Verlag AG Zürich

All rights reserved

English-language translation copyright © Stephen Brown 2020

The moral rights of the authors have been asserted

A CIP catalogue record for this book is available from the British Library

ISBN 978-1-912208-84-5
eISBN 978-1-912208-85-2

Typeset in Garamond by MacGuru Ltd
Printed in the UK by TJ International

All rights reserved.

This book has been supported by the Austrian Federal Chancellery.

⊒ Federal Chancellery
    Republic of Austria

Reinhold is the hero of my story.
Only because of him am I telling it.

Lucia Heilman

He was her father's best friend, at a time when men still had male best friends and women still had female best friends – half an eternity ago, that is. Reinhold Duschka and Rudolf Kraus. They must have met by chance back in the mid-1920s, after a lecture at the Palais Eschenbach or on a sunbathing lawn in the Lobau or on Duschka's first climbing trip with the Alpine Club to Peilstein in the southern Vienna Woods, that's how I imagine it: in a mountain hut or a jolting train compartment on the journey home, covered in grazes, bone-weary but happy to have had a new experience for which he could find no words, Duschka found himself sitting next to Kraus, who had led the group or accompanied it. It was Kraus's sober concern for the others that appealed to Duschka because it corresponded to his own nature.

For Duschka, the lowlander from Berlin, the urge upward into the mountains had been for the longest time alien. Or to be more precise, he had never given it a thought until a time he was traipsing through the Black Forest, more than six hundred kilometres from home, on his wanderings as a journeyman. He made a stop in Freiburg and, whether out of sheer Sunday boredom or because the name had a promising ring to it, he climbed the local mountain, Schauinsland ('View of the Country'), from which at sunset he laid eyes on the panorama of the Alps. To the south, on the horizon, light-blue jags under a pink-grey sky. Thus was his longing awoken.

Half a year later, in Vienna, Rudolf Kraus introduced Duschka to his circle of friends, who met regularly to discuss everything under the sun. *The Last Days of Mankind* and the Russian Revolution, German expressionism and Red Vienna, healthy nutrition and the Transparent Man, free love and technological progress – the conversation ran wild in all directions. Quite possible that, soon after, when the weather was bad or in the cold months of the year, they were meeting at 6 Pappenheimgasse in the Brigittenau district in a cramped and humble flat, which Regina Steinig – dark-haired and somewhat plump – shared with her father Josef Treister, a former gentleman landowner from a village near Trembowla, about one hundred and sixty kilometres southeast of Lemberg. After the outbreak of the First World War, Herr Treister and his wife had fled to Vienna with Regina and their sons Arnold and Julian. The head of the family could find only casual work in Vienna; perhaps, too, he could no longer muster the strength to build a new life for himself and his own, but he put everything into providing an academic education for his children.

The older he became, the more frequently Josef Treister sought solace for the trials of existence in religion. His wife, Anna, had died in 1921 from a haemorrhage in her womb caused by a fibroid; Arnold ran a thriving pharmacy in the city centre with a business partner; and of Julian little more was known than that he had become a wanted man for cardsharping and so fled abroad pell-mell. Regina, alone of her family and by a roundabout route, found out that her younger brother had settled in Lille, after several stops in between, and there had acquired money, a good reputation and apparently a family as well. Shortly after Julian's precipitate departure, the girlfriend he had left behind in Vienna gave birth to a girl, and Regina undertook to look after the young woman and her child, just as she had not hesitated to take in her indigent father. Arnold, her prosperous brother, had refused to have him, though there would have been ample room in the grand flat on Bäckerstraße where he had set up home with his wife, Cecylia. From time to time and only grudgingly he gave his sister money, which barely covered their father's outgoings, modest though they were.

Regina was the group's centre of gravity because she was gregarious by nature and had a knack for winning the trust of total strangers in an instant and then making them friends with each other. She was a doctor of chemistry, out of work like most in their circle, and officially she was still married to the lawyer Leon Steinig, who came from Trembowla like she did. They had fallen in love there when Regina was fourteen years old, before being separated by the events of the war. Assumed, that Steinig did his military service as a one-year volunteer and ended up in Vienna shortly before or after the dissolution of the Dual Monarchy. Their marriage, which was contracted soon after, lasted only a few years.

Faint clues that it was the tragic fate of their child that drove them apart: the child with whom the young couple had travelled to Galicia – part of Poland at the time – in the summer of 1923, six months after it was born, to see for themselves what had happened to the family home. The fields had been laid waste, buildings burned to the ground; sanitary conditions were abysmal. Bitter poverty of their relatives who had stayed behind. While they were staying in Trembowla, little Martin

Elia fell ill with dysentery and though they returned to Vienna with all speed, he died a few days later in the St. Anna children's hospital. A wound, which did not for a long time heal. Her husband responded to Regina's feelings of guilt with silence and ceaseless activity outside the home, first as general secretary of the World Union of Jewish Students, then as an official of the International Labour Organisation in Geneva. The first signs of their mutual estrangement: Steinig's flings, which she could not forgive because he denied them tenaciously to her face and boasted of them in front of others. Regina's incredulous astonishment when she came to hear that he had in the past betrayed her with her mother, a notable beauty, and then with her best friend.

Assumed, that the young wife was forced to rely on maintenance payments from her husband and besides thought it just that he should atone for his culpable behaviour. This would explain why she did not agree to a divorce until much later. By then, Steinig had long since been living permanently in Switzerland and came to Vienna only rarely, on the final occasion on a mission from the League of Nations to ask Sigmund Freud to debate with Albert Einstein, via an exchange of letters, whether there was a way to save humanity from the calamity of a new war. Freud, as we know, was sceptical and, as we also know, sadly proved right in his scepticism.

Whether because she lacked the money to have her identity documents modified or because she might have otherwise forfeited her Austrian citizenship, Regina continued to use the surname Steinig.

*

A circle of friends, then, half tending pacifist, half communist and for the most part with no need to affiliate to one party. While Regina's father sat on the edge of the bed in the room next door and read the Bible, they gathered around the kitchen table, a bowl in its centre, each receiving from their hostess a serving of cornmeal, which was filling and available cheap. At some point, as already mentioned, the lean and wiry Reinhold Duschka entered – chiselled features, rounded spectacles on a strong nose. He was silent most of the time but, when he did say something, the others in their surprise listened carefully. He had been apprenticed as a belt-maker in Berlin and from 1924 to 1928 studied in Josef Hoffmann's metalworking class at the Vienna School of Arts and Crafts, with secondary studies in life drawing and heraldry. Afterwards, he set himself up in business crafting bowls, vases, candlesticks, bracelets, ashtrays and animal figurines out of copper, brass and silver: original items within reach of those who valued the unique but could not afford luxury goods. Conceivable, that Reinhold was soon one of the few in their circle with a decent income at his disposal; certainly, he was able in 1929 to acquire or rent a plot of land in the 'allotment settlement' at Wolfersberg on a ninety-nine-year lease. With his then girlfriend Mina Gottlieb and an old college friend from the Hoffmann class, he built an 'allotment house' there based on his own designs: a cube with a flat roof and smooth façade, modest, straightforward in its interior decoration as well, in keeping with the ideas of his teacher.

In the same year, on 25 July, Regina gave birth to a girl to whom she gave the name Lucia. Rudolf Kraus was the father, proud and also willing to marry Regina, but she didn't want to know: nothing against Rudi, she is supposed once to have said, he's a decent man – conscientious, obliging, everything you'd want – but as a husband, he'd be intolerable. Two years later, when she finally obtained a position taking blood and testing blood sugar in the laboratory at the Lainz Hospital, she left her child under the supervision of its grandfather. Treister was already rather frail, and he put one foot only slowly in front of the other when he walked, but what he lacked in mobility he made good in warmheartedness, benevolence and patience; his stories of heaven and hell have long since been forgotten – not, however, the soft, deep tone of his voice, which enchanted her. Besides which, Rudi Kraus came to visit once a week, played or crafted things with her, or took her to his equally cramped apartment on Engerthstraße, which he shared with his mother and sister. No objection from Regina; on the contrary, they remained on cordial terms, even when, in 1932, she fell head over heels for the blond Fritz Hildebrandt, a carpenter from Franconia ten years her junior. No one else could find any use for this brainless fellow, who was lazy and unreliable to boot. It was a mystery what she saw in him. Perhaps not straightaway, but soon he moved in with her. Unforgotten still today, how he forced little Lucia to eat her plate clean when Regina was away. When she had to be sick as a result, he ordered her to wipe up the vomit.

For a few hours every Sunday morning, the mesh of relationships around her mother disentangled itself: while Rudi Kraus and Reinhold Duschka climbed a mountain together, Regina, Lucia and insipid Fritz Hildebrandt set off as a three on hikes into the Vienna Woods.

*

Meanwhile, Rudi Kraus had also found work: as an assistant assembler at Siemens-Schuckert. He studied mathematics at the university as a working student and completed his studies in 1936 with a doctorate. Lucia's scant recall of being present at his graduation: a ceremony with gowns and tasselled hats, speeches awkwardly fiery or well rehearsed, of which nothing remains in her memory.

A second and significantly sharper remembrance, of the doll Susi, which he had given her for her birthday, the torso of sackcloth and sawdust topped with a porcelain head, which at some point broke into pieces and was mended by her mother, only now its blue saucer eyes no longer closed when Lucia laid her dolly down to sleep.

A third memory, of her mother's wish that she call her Gina, which however she could never bring herself to say. Mummy!

The next, that she was allowed to fry Rudi's eggs, six cracked into the pan, which he devoured in one sitting.

Fifth memory, of Rudi's nice girlfriend Piroska Szabó, who was a dentist. Lucia's lower jaw was misaligned and Piroska fixed it for free or for a preferential rate.

Sixth, on her first day at school, her teacher's startled

look because the surnames of mother and daughter – Steinig, Treister – did not match and Lucia, to the enquiry after her father's name, gave the answer her mother had drilled into her and which stood also on her birth certificate: it is unknown.

Seventh memento, of holidays with her kind grandmother on Engerthstraße, the burning candles on the Christmas tree on Christmas Eve, an egg sprinkled with sugar on Easter Sunday.

Another memory, of her friend Erna Dankner in her flat on the ground floor. There is a photo of them sitting together on a blanket in front of a wooden fence with a ball, a balloon and a toy dog with floppy ears. Erna has her arm wrapped around Lucia's shoulders, and nothing about the two of them hints at the future circumstances in which, six or seven years hence, their life paths will cross once more, then be driven forever apart.

One more image from childhood: how Lucia walks hand in hand with her grandfather along the Danube Canal. It is shabbat or a major holiday, and the other pedestrians are festively dressed so that, for the first time, in her grey smock and her patched stockings, she feels shabby.

Not to forget the gatherings at Reinhold Duschka's summerhouse: as the sole child among noisy adults,

Lucia was bored or else pricked up her ears when the talk was of love affairs and quarrels, and Reinhold's girl-friend cooked peas and rice with exotic spices.

*

In 1937 she, Regina and, to Lucia's chagrin, Fritz Hildebrandt moved into a larger flat in the Ninth District: 29 Berggasse, Rear Building, 4th Floor. Now there was even a maid, who cooked for Lucia when she came home from school for lunch and, when the weather was good, went with her to Schlickpark, just a stone's throw away. Great excitement, because she once allowed the child, at her entreaty, to climb onto the windowsill: even if she held on tight, something still could have happened. Second and third excitement, Regina's well-founded suspicion that jaunty Fritz, who set every woman's heart aflutter, was making eyes behind her back at the maid and on top of that had begun an affair with a woman in the neighbourhood – whom Regina advised, emphatically, to keep her hands off.

Other than that, there were still the Sunday outings in the Vienna Woods, Duschka and Kraus's mountain climbs, gatherings in Regina's kitchen or at Reinhold's in Wolfersberg. Checking whether granddad needed anything, fetching him for dinner, begging for a story. Conversations about the impending catastrophe, which the adults feared but whose scale they did not foresee. Her mother's agitation, her jittery movements as Chancellor Schuschnigg announced on the radio that he had given way to force and entrusted the protection of Austria to a higher being, in whom she did not believe.

Eight-year-old Lucia, torn back and forth between panic and a craving for sensation, wanted, one Tuesday, to run towards Heldenplatz because everyone was running in that direction, but she became trapped in the crowds. Heil, heil, heil…! She sensed that she and her small family were excluded from the expected salvation, was frightened by the roaring masses in the street and came home distraught. And again, on 10 November, hearing that the Müllnergasse synagogue was on fire, she wanted to run to the scene of events. Her mother intercepted her at the door.

The Vienna municipality dismissed Regina as early as 14 May 1938, but required her to spend two weeks, unpaid, training her replacement, a woman with a silver-plated swastika dangling at her neckline. The maid stopped coming on the same day because she could no longer be expected to work in a Jewish household. Shortly after, Fritz rented a room for himself to avoid being denounced as a polluter of the race and, in the middle of May, Lucia was hounded out of junior school on Grünentorgasse and stuck into a school for Jewish children on Börsegasse. After a school day during which they learnt next to nothing on account of the over-crowded classrooms and lack of qualified teachers, she and her friends ran to Schlickpark. Her astonishment at the speed with which the warning FOR ARYANS ONLY had been painted onto every bench, beautifully uniform, stencilled. The girls switched to the street but, as they played hopscotch or with their skipping rope, they had to be constantly on the alert for teenagers who would spit on them and yank their hair. Eventually, in the summer, Josef Treister was thrown out of his flat on Pappenheimgasse. His daughter took him in. He had no one else; Arnold, the pharmacist, had by then already emigrated to Paris with his wife and child. He had had time to dispose of their possessions before-hand; Lucia was supposed to have received his daughter Renate's splendid doll's pram as a parting gift but, to Lucia's regret, Regina would have nothing to do with it.

And this is Lucia's last memory of her grandfather: how, on the evening of 9 September 1939, one week after the German attack on Poland, the doorbell rings and rings, men in boots are asking for Josef Treister, requesting that he come with them. How he packs a small suitcase and pulls on his heavy winter coat. How the door shuts behind him. How she runs to the window and sees him in the twilight between the strong, broad-shouldered men walking across the courtyard, small and bowed and with faltering steps, until he disappears into the passageway through the front building. He was imprisoned in the Vienna Stadium with over a thousand other men identified by the Nazi authorities as stateless Jews of Polish origin. Three or four days later, Regina and Lucia were standing in a queue in front of the building to hand in fresh underwear and warm clothing for him. Speaking was forbidden; uniformed men would beat anyone who disobeyed with clubs. To have to watch how they struck her mother because she has whispered to the woman in front of them, and to know that screaming or crying will only make things worse.

By the following week, when they wanted to deliver clean clothes to her grandfather again, he had already been transported away. A month later, a telegram from Buchenwald with the notification of death, cause of death unspecified: JOSEPH TREISTER BORN 16.3.73 DECEASED TODAY CREMATION ON 26.10.39 WEIMAR CREMATORIUM APPLICA-TION CONSIGNMENT OF ASHES AT OWN

COST TO BE ADDRESSED WITHIN 24 HOURS TO CEMETERY ADMINISTRATION WEIMAR CAMP COMMANDANT BUCHENWALD.

*

By this time, Fritz Hildebrandt was already a soldier in the German army, Piroska Szabó was on her way to Shanghai and Rudi Kraus was busy installing the lighting system for the newly built harness racing track in Tehran. He had applied for an overseas assignment after Austria was annexed, intending to have Regina and Lucia follow after him. But the outbreak of war scuppered his plan and when British and Soviet troops occupied Persia, he was interned as an enemy alien and then shipped with other detainees to Australia.

Before this, a university friend of Regina's, the chemist Erwin Tramer, had succeeded in obtaining an affidavit in the USA for her and Lucia, only Regina could find no one to advance her the money for the crossing. Regina had contemplated a third means of escape – sending her daughter to England on a Kindertransport – but when she discussed it with Lucia, the girl had immediately burst into tears. She did not want to be parted from her mother for anything in the world.

Mother and daughter had also travelled by train to Berlin, before the decree requiring that they wear the yellow star came into force, where a family was prepared to hide them in their home. Of their brief stay in the capital of the Reich, Lucia recalls only the Siegessäule and the Tiergarten and that, while her mother took a closer look at the particulars of the situation, she was left alone for an hour or so in the hands of a person who has since vanished from her memory.

Much too risky, Regina said when she came to collect her. The walls of the house are paper thin. You can hear every time the neighbours cough or flush the toilet.

Uncertain, whether the pair had by then already been forced to live in a 'collection flat' – fourteen people crammed into two and a half rooms, Regina and Lucia sharing a tiny box room with an elderly lady. One day a young married couple had rung the doorbell of their old flat on Berggasse, produced a warrant from the municipality of Vienna, inspected the rooms, judged them suitable, and had given Regina a fortnight to get out. Two beds complete with mattresses they were allowed to take with them; all other furniture was to be taken over by the new tenants without payment. Their new accommodation lay only one housing block away from their old flat, on the even-numbered side of the street;

midway between the two was a gap between buildings, where a kind of flea market took place. Possible, but not proven, that the girl may have roamed there with Erna Dankner, her friend from Pappenheimgasse, who had been assigned to the same building in a second 'collection flat' a floor below.

And the autumn of 1941 is approaching. Fritz – who the previous year had written a postcard from Paris in the giddy voice of the Blitzkrieg victor, I am writing you these lines from the Eiffel Tower – has long since been sent marching eastwards. Rudi Kraus has made it to Australia. Their relatives and circle of friends have been scattered across the world, disappeared or blended in. Only Lucia's grandmother on her father's side, the one on Engerthstraße, is still in the city – and her aunt Leopoldine, though she has by now married an SS man and does not want to be compromised by her brother's Jewish kin. The grandmother doesn't either, out of fear for her own life, and so no longer invites Regina and Lucia over to her house. Reinhold Duschka remains. He continues to meet with them, takes them to his allotment, now and then provides them with fruit and vegetables. Only the ice skating, which he had once been teaching the girl, has by now long been abandoned.

In one photo, taken in the last or second-to-last

summer before they went underground, Lucia is wearing a light-coloured summer dress and a hairband over her blonde curls, leaning on the balustrade of the balcony of his little 'allotment house'. She is smiling, as if she knew already of Reinhold's momentous decision, which he will communicate only to her mother, in monosyllables, as is his way. Regina thinks over his proposal calmly. She knows well how much is at stake for him, for her, for Lucia; having said that, it is high time for her to take up his offer. There have long been rumours that the 'Jewish houses' are being cleared, their occupants carried off in lorries. To where? To the place from which no one returns.

*

A parenthesis, unavoidable for the progress of the story: ten years earlier, Reinhold Duschka had taken a lease at the so-called Werkstättenhof ('Workshop Court'), a magnificent industrial building between Linker Wienzeile, Hornbostelgasse and Mollardgasse erected in 1908 for the sixtieth jubilee of the reign of Emperor Franz Joseph. A hundred and fifty businesses were distributed over six storeys on three sides of a large inner courtyard; the fourth, eastern side was occupied by a long block of flats reserved for the craftsmen and women and their families. Every workshop had a heavy iron door and, on account of the weight and vibrations from the machinery, every floor was built of reinforced concrete T-beams and the interior walls were soundproofed.

Every day, several hundred people entered and left – artisans, suppliers, service engineers, messengers, customers – and with them carts, wagons and lorries. Who there paid attention to a plump woman and a skinny girl scurrying up the broad staircase to the fourth floor on three consecutive days, into Reinhold's workshop, with its windows looking out onto Hornbostelgasse and Vienna's Industrial Trade School opposite? Thus they managed to carry their last worldly goods into the Werkstättenhof, packed into inconspicuous bags: clothes, shoes, bed linen, a sewing basket, soap, two combs, four toothbrushes, a few photos and books, a pencil case with crayons, the board game 'Hey, Don't Get Angry!', a small jigsaw, four or five gouges, a wooden handle and a roller for linocuts and the bears Bam, Bem, Bim and Augustin.

As they are returning home on the third day, they are already walking down Berggasse when Regina suddenly stops and grasps Lucia by the hand. She has seen the lorry in front of their building, now the girl spots it too, and they are not the only passers-by watching what is happening. Just now, the inmates of the two 'collection flats' are being driven out of the front door of the block and to the rear of the vehicle where they climb one by one up a ladder set against it and onto the load bed. In Lucia's memory the process lasts only a few seconds. Or half a minute, a whole minute. The people are standing crammed together in the back of the lorry and suddenly something happens, about which Lucia is unsure whether she saw it with her own eyes, simply imagined it, or heard about it from her mother's telling: Erna Dankner, who is standing right on the edge of the group, clamped between her companions in misery and the right side panel of the lorry, loses her balance at the exact moment the lorry moves forward, sways, plunges onto the street and appears – it is impossible to see clearly at that distance – to be run over by one of the rear wheels. Her inert body, screams, tumult; swiftly Regina pulls her daughter into a side street.

Don't turn around, she says. We're taking the tram on the corner up ahead.

Moments later, Lucia is standing next to her mother on the open deck of the tram – it is forbidden for Jews to stay in the interior of the carriage – staring at the roadway. What is going through her head then she will, decades later, be unable to recall. They have to change once; after half an hour they are at Margaretengürtel. As they walk across the bridge over the Wien river, Regina presses her handbag against her chest, Lucia hides her star with her scarf. They enter the Werkstättenhof by the side entrance on Hornbostelgasse. It is, we imagine, early afternoon. The stairwell is deserted. At one point they hear the rumbling of the goods lift. Then Regina is pressing the doorbell. This night will become, earlier than planned, the first that mother and daughter spend at Reinhold's place of work, their precarious home for the next four years, the story of which remains to be told.

*

First, however, we must describe the workshop, starting from the iron door, which has snapped shut behind them, and the short, windowless hallway, at the end of which two brown-painted doors stand open. The door to the right takes you into the workshop proper, a large space of sixty or even eighty square metres with two windows of reinforced glass and iron glazing bars taking up almost the whole width of the outside wall; the door on the left leads to a second room, six metres by five, in which Reinhold has until today displayed examples of his range and which will remain closed to customers and other visitors from now on. Here, too, a window with glazing bars ensures there is ample daylight. A rectangular table stands in front of the window, a large round table stands in the middle of the room, heaped with samples, and against the rear wall is a sort of shed in the form of a long crate, one metre fifty tall, four metres wide and ninety centimetres deep, which Reinhold has carpentered from laths and planks and fastened to the wall with angle irons. A store for tools, cardboard boxes and canisters, you would think, but anyone who presses on the hatch at the left-hand end of the crate, which is half-obscured by a low shelf of ten, fifteen books, will see that Reinhold has laid out two mattresses end-to-end on the floor of the shed: sleeping quarters for mother and daughter.

Hard to imagine that the two of them could bear being in that narrow, airless hiding place together for long; and indeed after some weeks or months Reinhold hauls in an Inrusa brand camp bed, which someone gave him or let him have on the cheap. Every evening it is unfolded for Lucia, the next morning it is cleared away into their crate with the bed linen. While Regina relieves herself into a bucket, Lucia walks with her sponge, hand towel and soap across into the workshop – with its peculiar smell of soldering grease, polishing compound and stale air, which is still familiar to her seventy or more years later – weaves her way between the workbench, the cast-iron oven, the long work table with several sheets of metal beneath it, and the broad cabinet, where finished goods made for stock stand behind glass, on through to the sink, a large metal trough for patinating, dyeing and washing materials. To its left, the soldering table, burner and gas stove. She puts on the kettle. By the time Reinhold arrives a little after eight, she and her mother are already at work. Six days a week, Monday to Saturday.

*

On the consequences of their flight the adults wasted not a word. Reinhold remained silent because he only ever spoke when he thought it unavoidable anyway and Regina because she did not want to frighten Lucia – the both of them because talk of danger would do nothing to avert it. They had seen enough in any case to imagine how the authorities would react to their disappearance. It was probable that the two of them had not even been recorded as missing when the others from their 'collection flat' were delivered to a transit camp in the Second District. Their absence would only have attracted attention when Regina did not comply with a written summons to make herself and her daughter available for collection. At that point, Gestapo spies would have put the building that had housed the now cleared 'collection flats' under observation for a few days, at the same time hunting for them in the district and in those businesses where Jews were still allowed to shop – most likely in a careless and desultory fashion since those who went underground generally ran into the police sooner or later anyway, at a road block or during a raid, or were rooted out of their hiding place thanks to a tip-off or sometimes in the course of another operation. Hard to imagine in such circumstances that the Gestapo would have become aware of Reinhold Duschka; but it could not be ruled out. The police could have questioned someone who knew of his friendship with Regina Steinig, and he or she, whether all too hastily or under threat of a beating or after a prolonged and brutal interrogation, named his name. They would have tailed Reinhold for several days then searched his house without warning. At his home, they would have found nothing. But the hiding place in the spare room of his workshop would not have escaped their practised gaze.

This was one reason why they lived in constant fear. Another lay in the fact that Regina and Lucia depended on Reinhold's presence and his health. If something happened to him, they were lost. Regina knew no one else who could have taken them into their home or sheltered them elsewhere, in the basement of a suburban villa, in an 'allotment cottage', in the back room of a junk shop. And even if by some miracle they could have found a new hiding place, it would scarcely have been possible to feed them. Rations were being cut back each year, so it would have taken ten or twelve ration card holders to provide for two additional people. A network of helpers then, foolhardy and cool-headed at the same time.

Although the three of them had to manage on the food ration cards of one, Reinhold was rarely at a loss about where to get the next day's food. As the war wore on, demand for handcrafted goods rose, goods whose appearance and use provided people for a short time with the feeling that they were living in a time of peace. With Lucia and Regina as his semi-skilled assistants, he could manufacture more pieces and procure food on the black market with the extra revenue. They knew that a grocer secretly sold him goods that would otherwise have had to be purchased with coupons.

Will he not be suspicious, if you keep on showing up at his shop? asked Regina once.

No chance, responded Reinhold. I've told him I'm an elite athlete and so I'm always hungry.

Reinhold was a regular at the Naschmarkt too, fifteen minutes from the Werkstättenhof. There, farmers from the surrounding area sold whatever vegetables they hadn't been made to surrender. He was there once when a load of carrots came in; he brought a huge sackful on a trolley into the workshop where they ate them for weeks: raw, shredded, cooked. Meat, on the other hand, was so scarce as to be all but unaffordable. For Reinhold that was neither here nor there – he ate an almost exclusively vegetarian diet – but Lucia was still growing and needed balanced nutrition, even though, unlike her mother, she has been a 'small eater' all her life, as she puts it, and already was back then.

There was a time, however, right at the beginning, in the first week after they had gone to ground, when Reinhold was unable to provide them with sufficient food. As a result, says Lucia, her mother went outside, alone, without her yellow badge or identity card, to use a telephone box to call a neighbour in the building at 29 Berggasse, a woman who had seen no reason after the Anschluss to treat a Jew and her daughter as enemies. The woman was immediately willing to help Regina with a loaf of bread. Unknown where they met, in a church or passage perhaps. The neighbour asked her no questions; the less she knew, the less risk for her. Though Regina was afraid the whole time that her former patients from the Lainz Hospital might recognise her in the street, the two women must have seen each other at a later date as well, or at any rate spoken on the phone, because Lucia remembers her mother saying that their neighbour's son, fighting as a soldier in the German army, had fallen at Stalingrad. Her only child, said Regina. She was in despair, distraught. After that, for reasons that remain mysterious, there was no further contact between her mother and the woman.

Lucia's grandmother knew that they had gone underground, but where and with whom Regina withheld from her. Fritz Hildebrandt, by contrast, knew the secret; he even visited them at Reinhold's workshop when he came to Vienna on leave from the front or because he needed hospital treatment for a recurrent furunculosis. Though Reinhold couldn't bear him, Lucia says, he didn't think him capable of betrayal.

Two further people had it in their power to set the authorities on Regina's trail. The first was a consultant or chief physician at the Lainz Hospital, for whose research Regina had once determined the vitamin content of Hungarian paprika and the glucose content of lacrimal fluid. Possible, that Regina had already sought his help in August 1939, when the conscription board was considering men from the 1900 age cohort for the first time. Reinhold was short-sighted, he ran a one-man business, he had no experience of the front, his profession in no way suited him to the purposes of the military. Still, there was a danger he would be declared fit for service. And within the following year, by the aftermath of the offensive against the Soviet Union at the latest, he would surely have been called up for military service or conscripted into strategically important work, had Regina and her acquaintance from the hospital not intervened. Regina with a mix of pills – an entire phial full, as Lucia remembers it – which Reinhold gulped down the evening before each medical; the doctor by recommending them to a senior colleague in the medical arm of the German Air Force, bound to him by friendship and, in his estimation, entirely trustworthy. Of him, Lucia retains only his name, Doctor Rudolf Mader, that he lived on Albertgasse and that he was prepared to issue a certificate attesting that Reinhold had a congenital heart defect. In return, Mader received each time a gift: a vase, a pot and cup – on one occasion a rug, which Reinhold had acquired during his studies at the School of Arts and Crafts and from which he now parted with a light heart.

On the days when Reinhold had to appear before the medical panel, says Lucia, she and her mother were always in fearful anxiety. Only when he had walked back in through their door smiling did their agitation subside.

She no longer knows when they fled to Reinhold in his workshop. Was it 1941 or only the beginning of 1942? She does not recall the season: was there snow on the ground? No. Were the trees in bloom or had they lost their leaves? Could be. Was there summer's heat? Possibly. Actually, no, she was wearing a coat and scarf when they walked across the bridge to the Werkstättenhof that last time. Besides, it was there that she heard, on Reinhold's People's Radio, not only the scolding voices of Hitler and Goebbels but also the reports of the rapid advances of the German combat units deep into enemy territory. The Army Group Centre is thirty kilometres from Moscow! She can remember the jubilant tone of a man's voice at this news and she believes she heard her mother crying out in horror: but that's no further than we are from Baden!

A day in November 1941, therefore. At this moment,

Lucia was twelve years and four months old and was filing smooth a square coaster made of copper sheet. She hated this task because it was monotonous and demanded neither imagination nor dexterity. You had to grip the millimetre-thick sheet between two protective layers in a vice, work on the edges with a coarse file, then progressively finer ones, before a final polish with sandpaper. Almost always Reinhold would send the piece back, twice, five or ten times. It's uneven here, and here, go over it one more time with the finest file.

He showed me how to do it over and over again. He was affectionate; he never told me off, never lost patience.

At soldering the girl worked so skilfully from the beginning that he soon left her to it. At most, he helped fix the pieces in place with clamps before Lucia set about using a blowpipe and bellows to solder on a handle, a base, a ring stand, small feet or, in particularly large quantities because it was a popular Christmas gift, a screw in the centre of a decorative stopper, which could then be screwed into the cork of a wine bottle. You had to move quickly, get the temperature right and not let the thin tin plate begin to trickle, and it required a calm hand, a precise eye.

There was good fortune even in the bad: that Regina

and Lucia had to work in order to stay alive. The work steadied them, distracted them, offered them the chance to show their gratitude for Reinhold's audacity. For Lucia, it meant diversion and contemplation at the same time, a kind of security, and that was above all thanks to him.

She liked that he was always coming up with something new. Aside from the decorative stoppers, which were quick to make, and the bracelets, for which they used up leftovers from a sheet of brass, no one piece resembled another. One vase was pointed, the next bulbous, the next after that triangular. Add to that the ease with which Reinhold brought into being a horse or a swan with nothing more than a pair of pliers and a slender strip of metal – and his modesty: he did not insist on his authority. He gave out advice, not orders. Although he reserved the really difficult tasks for himself, he enabled them to take part in the entire process of manufacture, which usually encompassed a dozen steps. Marking out lines with a lead pencil. Cutting out with tin snips. Smoothing with a wooden mallet. Blocking with six or seven other hammers, delivering targeted blows at regular intervals from the centre out towards the rim until the metal begins to take on a particular shape. Sinking, annealing over the flame of a Bunsen burner, quenching in a trough of dilute sulphuric acid, rinsing, raising on a squared timber or one of the two tree stumps, smooth or indented, that stood next to the workbench, planishing, deburring and polishing. Finally, the soaring moment when a piece of work, checked over by Reinhold one more time, held up to the light and rotated, was then put away into the cupboard.

In the early days, there was still copper. Sometimes, infrequently, silver. When there was no more copper to be had, we worked with Zinkal, an alloy of zinc and aluminium. It was a really poor material; after a bit it mottled. We polished it so you couldn't see the spots and patinated it to give it a brownish appearance. After a couple of months, it was mottled again. But there were no complaints. In the war, no one complained because they were glad to have anything at all.

The hammering went on all day until they had to switch on the lights: two bare light bulbs that hung from the ceiling over the workbench and the table. Before that, Reinhold would pull down the black roller blinds. His hand movement has stuck in Lucia's memory, how he meticulously stroked the rolls of paper so they overlapped at the edges because a strict blackout had been decreed and the air raid warden checked for compliance from the street. Later, for similar reasons,

Reinhold had to set a bucket of sand by the front door for fighting fires in the event of an air raid, a feeble precaution, which Regina poked fun at. She mocked the cartoons in *Der Stürmer*, too, when Reinhold once brought home a copy; unknown, who had foisted it upon him. Infected with her gallows humour, he told a couple of bitterly angry jokes that he had picked up somewhere. What stands out in Lucia's memory is not that the jokes made a mockery of the Nazis in their Jew-hatred, but that Reinhold had, for once, without being prompted or required by the situation, uttered more than two sentences.

My mother was a chatterbox; she loved to talk. Reinhold just threw in a word here and there. And I – I agonised over what I could say.

Twice a day, at midday and towards evening, Regina prepared a meal, which they would consume on the worktable, where there was just enough room. A happy chance that the doorbell never rang while she was cooking. Mostly it rang in the morning, and every time for one terrified moment mother and daughter would be as if turned to stone. Then, in a flurry, they would race to gather up anything that could betray their presence – a cardigan, an apron, Lucia's family of bears for whom she'd built a street on the floor out of scraps of metal and wood – and then run across into the other room, close the door behind them and crawl into their crate, as they called their hiding place. Silent, not even whispering to each other, sometimes fighting down a tickling cough as well, they crouched on the mattresses until Reinhold had finished with the visitors. Apart from postmen, they were mostly suppliers, craftspeople from the same floor borrowing hammers or clamps, or a woman from the first floor who ran an enamelling studio and often had commissions from Reinhold. In the afternoon, usually only customers came. That paralysing terror every time someone rang the bell had shadowed Lucia since the day the doorbell had rung on Berggasse and they had opened the door and men had stamped into their flat to lead her grandfather away.

There was danger even when Regina or Lucia needed to go to the toilet. In Reinhold's absence, at night or on Sundays when he was away mountaineering, they used a bucket, but during working hours, once Reinhold had convinced them there was no one in sight, they dashed out into the corridor to one of the two shared toilets provided on each storey. Astonishing that they were never discovered in the process.

Work continued for a little while by artificial light, tasks that didn't cause much noise, such as the filing

Lucia detested. Around six o'clock in the evening, seven at the latest, Reinhold said his goodbyes and locked the door from the outside. The spare key hung on a hook next to the door.

His life outside the workshop remained hidden from them. Lucia did not know where he lived, whether he met up with friends, had a steady girlfriend, who he climbed with on Sundays or where. Perhaps he and Regina had a silent agreement to leave his private life blank in their conversations, and the girl never thought to ask him. Much of the time she paid no attention to what the adults said. She longed for children to play with or watch playing. She thought constantly about the children at the Trade School across the street. Time and again she was tempted to walk up to the window so that she could glance into their classrooms, see the faraway rows of benches, the heads, shoulders, arms of people her age or a little older who sometimes whispered secretly to each other, stood up, opened the windows for fresh air or walked forward to the blackboard, which remained hidden from her. She remembers her mother's warning cry: Not so close! Get back! She remembers the tears that ran over her cheeks as she stood and looked.

*

It was never really properly clean. Each evening they brushed away the shavings and Regina swept the floor. The windows were covered in filth, which no one disturbed; the walls were grey with soot. When Lucia woke one night with itchy bites on her arms and belly and began to scratch herself like a maniac, they went on the hunt for bedbugs. After a long search, they discovered that the vermin had lodged themselves in the coil springs of the folding bed and so tried to squash them with wooden sticks. Lucia remembers the fearsome stink that rose up as they killed them. When this failed to eradicate the bugs, Reinhold attacked with a killer spray, dousing them with the strong-smelling liquid several times a day for several days, until finally they were left in peace.

In the cold months, the oven never went out. When there were no more briquettes to be had, they burned scraps of wood, cardboard, wastepaper, whatever was available. That too was fortunate, that they were never cold, not even the first winter after they went underground, which was especially severe. Regina did their washing in the big sink, then hung it out to dry next to the oven overnight. Over time their underwear, skirts and stockings were fit only as rags. Lucia grew out of her clothes. But to use the points on his clothing card to buy women's underwear and children's shoes was a risk Reinhold could not take. He asked around his climbing friends, among whom, Lucia is convinced, there were young women who idolised him. Perhaps one of them helped out in a parish and gave him skirts and shoes discarded by benevolent churchgoers. Regina was glad she had never much cared about her wardrobe. And Lucia had no pretensions anyway. Most of the time she wore a man's shirt with the sleeves rolled up and fastened around the waist with a cord, in winter thick woollen socks or puttees of threadbare cloth and clogs instead of shoes, wooden soles onto which Reinhold had nailed fabric straps.

Her first menstruation did not frighten her. Regina had enlightened her daughter in good time and in a way that had awakened neither suspense nor revulsion; now that it had happened, the ache in her belly was painful but trivial set against the steady subliminal fear of discovery. The only part Lucia found unpleasant was the procedure she had already witnessed her mother performing: catching the blood with scraps of cloth, which from time to time they had to wash out. Sanitary towels or paper liners, difficult enough for anyone to get hold of, were beyond even Reinhold's ingenuity.

On Sundays, a deathly quiet reigned over the

Werkstättenhof. Not even the porter, while there still was one, was in the building. In spite of the thick walls and massive floors, work was unthinkable: noises from Reinhold's workshop, which was otherwise indistinguishable from the rest, might have made a chance visitor suspicious or alerted the air raid warden, if he happened one weekend to trudge up the stairwell to inspect the buckets of sand. They could use no light because the meter in the hall would have run, nor could they go to the toilet because the flushing might have betrayed them.

For Lucia, this was the day on which she plunged herself into a world of beguiling adventures and unbreakable friendships. Reinhold had enrolled himself into a lending library for her sake and rarely forgot to supply her with something new to read. Thus she journeyed to the moon and to the centre of the Earth, accompanied Michael Strogoff on his perilous mission to Irkutsk, wept for the beautiful Nscho-tschi – and even more for her gallant brother – and hated Fräulein Raimar with her boarding school for young ladies from the bottom of her heart. Regina, who read little, would try from time to time to begin a conversation, then let it drop because her daughter answered her either not at all or only after half a minute. What did you say,

Mummy? They went to bed early. Their anxious eyes on the door, early on Monday morning, as the key turned in the lock.

*

Here was something else for which Lucia gave him great credit: that in such difficult circumstances, tolerable only if the days ran as smoothly as possible, Reinhold instinctively recognised how much her confinement weighed upon her and so was always devising new tasks. In the second cupboard, which stood in the workshop against the wall with the adjoining room, there were compartments and drawers for sheets of paper, pencils, sharpeners, rubbers, coloured ribbons and packaging material. A typewriter was stored there too, covered with a leather hood, and Reinhold fetched it out whenever there were invoices and delivery notes to be raised. He showed Lucia how the letter paper, carbon and manifold had to be laid one on top of the other and fed round the roller, where the recipient's name and address should go, where the date belonged, where the subject line, which words had to be underlined or written in capitals by turning the platen upwards and locking the shift key. He wrote out the letters for her by hand in block capitals, she set about her work with a passion. Beginner's errors inserting the carbon paper thwarted her. Either it slipped or she fed it in incorrectly, with the coated side facing upwards, so that the characters appeared not on the manifold paper but in reverse on the back of the letter paper. She made frequent typing errors or forgot to use the correct spacing. Reinhold insisted that she get into the habit of carefully reading over every letter one more time, before presenting it to him to be checked.

Preparing orders became another challenge for Lucia's ambition. She pushed the chair up against the glass cabinet, on top of which stood the cardboard boxes purchased by Reinhold from a cardboard maker in the building. She climbed onto the chair, stretched herself until she could reach one of the boxes with her fingertips, then she and Regina packed the pieces into it, wrapped in tissue paper. They stuffed the gaps with wood shavings, laid the list of items on top, closed the flaps and wrapped the box in brown paper. The final step was tying the packages up with string. Lucia learned that the twine would remain tautly tensioned as you knotted it provided that you looped it and then pulled it through the loop. Reinhold did the labelling; a child's script could have made someone suspicious.

There was no chivvying, says Lucia. I was never put under too much pressure. Whether and how long I worked was left to me. If I was weary of hammering, I tapped out a letter or two. Then I looked for something to read or helped my mother peeling carrots. Gouged something out of lino or used a fretsaw to saw out a figure.

She found instructions for her projects in the handicraft pages of a children's magazine, which still used to come out every fortnight for the first months after they went underground – until the publishing house was denied a paper ration and had to cease publication. The title of the magazine has slipped Lucia's mind; it was something to do with an animal, she says. *Butterfly?* No. *The Parrot?* Not that either. *Lapwing?* I can't remember.

She followed the instructions to the letter. Even with the painting of the designs she did not trust herself to choose alternative colours. The conjecture that she tried to follow the instructions to the point of compulsion because of the constant danger she was in, that it seemed to keep her safe, Lucia does not accept. She was simply not artistically gifted, she says, that was clear to her already as a child. Whenever she drew something, it never came out the way she had envisaged it. Unlike her mother, who had no interest in such things, she had learned handicrafts at school. One day she set about crocheting tiny woollen coats for her bears. The disappointment later, when she realised that not one of them had really come out right. She fared better another time with the small exercise books she crafted for them out of cord and paper. Each one would receive a book clamped under its arm before being sent off by Lucia to the school for bears.

As involuntary and unwished-for home tutor to her daughter, Regina was in a hopeless position. Even to give a lesson required coaxing her daughter for half an hour first. Once Lucia had finally agreed to open a book or exercise book, there was always the danger that the girl might jump up under some pretext to run across into the other room, or decide it was more important that she work alongside Reinhold. At such moments, even filing was suddenly welcome to Lucia. No matter if it was about fractions, the distinction between adverbs and adjectives, the speed of light or the four types of chemical compound – it all entered one ear and left through the other. That her mother was, as Lucia says, rather impatient by temperament did not improve things. Scolding didn't help. Besides, the question pressed itself on Lucia whether it was worth learning anything at all. To what purpose? For when? For the longest time, it seemed to her that she would never again be among other people. One night she became terrified when she realised how hazy her image already was of sitting in a classroom among high-spirited, helpful, mischievous children, next to a girl who shields her exercise book with her left hand every time they have to do a dictation, in front of another who places a slip of paper for her, folded many times, onto the bench, on which are the words: Will you be my friend?

After four years at primary school, Lucia had transferred to a Jewish secondary school, the Chajes Gymnasium, but the authorities had closed it down in the middle of October 1939, just a month after the beginning of the school year. For the entrance examination, they had had to retell the story of the tailor, his three good sons and the dishonest nanny goat, and furnish it with a new title. Lucia had written: 'Everyone has to know how to help themselves.' Now she often had the feeling – constantly, in fact – that of the three of them only Reinhold knew how to help himself and others. He was the only one who never seemed anxious. If his mood changed, he did not show it, did not lose his saintly patience. Yes, there was once an argument, when Regina absolutely insisted on opening one of the jars of stewed fruit that stood on the bookshelf in the spare room as a kind of emergency reserve, and he was vehemently opposed.

Reinhold tried to teach her school knowledge as well. With the atlas open in front of them, they studied the continents, oceans, great mountain ranges and rivers, the nations and capitals of Europe. For this, Lucia was able to muster more interest; firstly because it helped her whenever she played 'City – Country – River' against him, secondly because it enabled her to orientate herself better on the map that Reinhold had stuck onto the glass-fronted cabinet. It was not until a year and a half after their flight into the workshop that she began to mark out the fronts on the map with small coloured pennants. For as long as the German armed forces were occupying one country after another, it had been impossible to think about. Back then she would have preferred to smash the radio set to pieces because the news reports drove her mother to despair. How will it all end? That deep groan rings in Lucia's ears to this day.

Hearing the words with which Regina one day made her last requests was even worse. She lay in their hideaway in a high fever, short of breath and shivering, vomited up the soup Reinhold had cooked and responded neither to a vinegar poultice nor to the flu remedies from the medicine cabinet. Lucia cannot remember whether they persisted, even for just an hour at a time, with their normal working life, except of course without her mother; whether Reinhold went home in the evening or stayed overnight in the workshop to look after Regina, on the second, now unoccupied, mattress in their crate. Nor can she say whether the adults wanted to take the risk of summoning a doctor, whether they dismissed the thought having barely considered it or were torn apart by the question and in their indecision delayed long enough to convince Regina that medical help would be too late to help her in any case but might still put Lucia and Reinhold at risk. Little to tell, therefore, of the progress of her illness, her closeness to death, nothing really apart from Regina's instruction that they should dismember her corpse in the workshop and bury it secretly in Reinhold's allotment.

You will do it, Reinhold. Promise me. And please, see her through. A last request, with no legal witness.

*

They never had fun. (Not even Reinhold, though he looked like an elf.) They never celebrated birthdays, Christmas, New Year's Eve. (And there were no presents either.) She never saw any tenderness growing between her mother and Reinhold. (I would have noticed. A child has a sixth sense for that kind of thing. Besides, I was dreadfully jealous of my mother.) She also never noticed her mother and Fritz Hildebrandt retreating into the spare room, or that they were in there alone for considerable periods every time he visited. (I would have noticed. A child has a sixth sense…) She does not know whether her mother hugged her, but she says with certainty that she cried on her mother's breast. (Because I remember her shoulder was above me, so actually she must have taken me in her arms.) She played Battleships and 'Hey, Don't Get Angry!' with Reinhold. He always let her win. (Apart from the first time, and then I was so enraged I sent the counters flying.) She played the same record, Schubert's *Unfinished Symphony*, for hours at a time on his gramophone (which sat in the spare room on the large round table with the display pieces). She voluntarily memorised Schiller's 'Song of the Bell' – all nineteen verses. She owned a friendship book, with a green binding and a gold-coloured lock. Sometimes she got hold of it, opened it, flicked through the empty pages. (I wanted to write something in it. But I didn't know what. I hadn't experienced anything. I never met anyone.)

Lucia begged to be allowed out. They gave in to her entreaties only three, at most four times, she maintains. Ahead of time, the adults drilled into her what she should say if someone stopped and questioned her. Why are you not in school? Where exactly do you live? What are your parents called? Do you have brothers and sisters? How come you're so pale? Are you on your own? She was convinced she would not betray herself, would parry every trick question, would rather let herself be tortured to death than confess who she was and with whom she was hiding. Besides which, they headed out as a pair, she and Reinhold, after she had put on a pleated skirt from her collection of old clothes and slipped into the only pair of shoes that even half fitted her. They walked down the staircase, Lucia four or five steps ahead so that none of Reinhold's neighbours in the Werkstättenhof might get the idea that they were together. Only on the pavement of Hornbostelgasse did she come to a stop, squint in the sunlight and wait for him to catch up with her. They walked up Gumpendorfer Straße, caught the metro at the Gürtel and changed onto the tram at Nußdorfer Straße.

Lucia wanted to store everything she saw in her memory, but that wish itself thwarted her plan: she inspected everything so intensely that she straightaway forgot whatever she had thought was worth remembering. Dirty grey façades with arrows pointing downwards, a fountain shrouded in bricks, a cinema playbill for *Rembrandt* with Ewald Balser in the lead role, a poster of three men drinking beer in front of a threatening-looking shadow. A coachman pummelled his weary horses. Two chattering girls, smaller than her, with school satchels on their backs and a boy her age in a brown Hitler Youth shirt carrying a shoebox with holes in it under his arm. A war invalid on one leg and two crutches leaned against the balustrade of the platform; a soldier stared at a woman conductor, who cadged a cigarette off him, brazenly, as unrestrained as her bosom. Two old women quarrelled noisily, coarse words over a place to sit.

In Grinzing, at the end of the line, Reinhold and Lucia strode away from the city between low vintner's houses and wine taverns. At the end of the village, they turned left onto a side path that led steeply uphill between vineyards. Shortly before where the path joined Höhenstraße was a bench made of weathered planks and a slender rusted frame. From here they had a broad, uninterrupted view over the city, the river and the outskirts to the east. But for this and for Reinhold's explanations of which tower or dome belonged to which building, Lucia had at that moment no time.

She kicked off her shoes, pulled off her stockings and charged away along the well-worn path next to the road; he watched her slender form grow rapidly smaller until it disappeared behind the trees or a bush. At the junction with Himmelstraße she turned around and hurtled back, running in the opposite direction, due north, past Reinhold, who in the meantime had pulled Rilke's *Book of Images* out of his jacket pocket. Lucia had discovered this slim volume a long time ago on the shelf next to their den and, as with all printed matter she got her hands on, wolfed it down greedily.

After a few hundred metres, she turned and ran back past Reinhold again. And so she went, four, five or six times back and forth, a girl in motion; now to the left, now to the right. Sometimes a military lorry or limousine rumbled across the Höhenstraße and, on the flank of the Latisberg on the far side of the road, sat the Cobenzl Schloßhotel, which she was under no circumstances to approach, he had drummed this into her, because it was being used as a military hospital, perhaps even as the command centre of the Vienna anti-aircraft brigade. After half an hour, a heated Lucia flopped onto the bench next to him; now they pointed out and named to each other the landmarks of the city they could see in the shimmering haze.

Even as they were descending, Lucia fretted that her inattention might spoil her precious time outdoors. She would have loved nothing more than to absorb everything around her or wrap it up so that she could live off it for as long as possible after. The twittering of birds, the wind in her hair, the smell of freshly cut grass. Hastily she plucked wildflowers for a posy, which to her seemed bedraggled and to its recipient Regina magnificent. She retained her exhilaration into the following morning, when she sprang out of the folding bed in high spirits in spite of her aching muscles. On their return home, just when Reinhold had unlocked the door, a man had stepped out into the corridor from the cabinetry workshop next door, but to their relief he had looked in the other direction. Or was that just how it seemed to them?

*

Presumed, that this excursion took place between May and September 1943. It would have been the last time the two of them ventured out of the workshop together. Snow lay on the Cobenzl for most of the winter; it was too cold for running around, and besides, the naked boughs of the trees and vines offered no shield from prying eyes. And then, before the snow melted, the air raids on Vienna began; hard to imagine that Regina would have indulged her daughter's compulsion to move after that.

Long before then, however, on an evening in late autumn or winter 1942, they must have gone out as a three because Lucia sees herself and Reinhold standing in front of a building on Albertgasse, their breath steaming, waiting for Regina, who has gone in to see Colonel Doctor Mader in his flat about Reinhold's certification and it is likely this time that she has brought him the carpet as a gift; that would explain why all three of them have left the workshop: Regina to call on the doctor, Reinhold to carry the rolled-up carpet, Lucia because her mother wanted under no circumstances to leave her alone. So Reinhold and she are standing in the gloom in front of the building, shifting from one foot to the other and talking in muted voices about the battle of Stalingrad, which has been going on for weeks. The German army is surrounded, the Germans are going to lose the war: this or a similar sentence Lucia hears herself saying grandly, and in fact she will soon be able to pin out on her map the so-called 'straightening of the front' in the east announced by Reich Broadcasting Vienna, as she will later the surrender of the Afrika

Korps in Tunisia and the landing of the allied forces in Sicily the following year.

Over a year later, from March 1944 when Vienna was bombed for the first time, they would turn on the radio each morning. At eleven, the cuckoo would call seven times, which meant that enemy forces were approaching – bomber squadrons from the US air force – and one hour later, almost to the minute, the sky over the city would be overrun. Regina reacted with terror, Lucia with a burst of satisfaction at this new threat: now the Nazis will get it in the neck! During the air raids, unseen by them, empty trams and buses stood between rows of buildings. Here and there a laden cart missing its horses, which had been unharnessed in a rush and stabled in the entranceway of a building. The classrooms in the school opposite had emptied themselves immediately after the early warning; this they did not witness either. Only once they were crouched in their crate did Reinhold run down into the air-raid shelter. Perhaps he opened a window beforehand, so that the panes would not be shattered by the blast wave, turned off the gas tap and hung up the rucksack containing emergency provisions, a torch and bandages. He didn't like to leave the two of them in the workshop, behind a door that regulations required be unlocked during the alert, but in the long run it would have been difficult for him to justify his absence from the cellar.

The piercing wail of the sirens sounded especially dreadful to Lucia, so that still today the factory knocking-off siren every Saturday at midday goes right into her bones, vibrates in her memory alongside other death-heralding sounds: the drone of the aeroplanes, the bark of the anti-aircraft guns, the hissing and whining of the bombs plummeting from the sky, their numbing crash. At first they fell only on the outer districts, on factories, workers' barracks, airfields and refineries on the far side of the Danube and in the south of the city, but soon they were hitting army barracks near the centre, railway stations and tracks and, from the summer onwards, residential housing in the central districts. It was only a matter of time before the neighbourhood between Wienzeile and Mariahilfer Straße would be bombed. Still Regina did not dare to visit the cellar with Lucia. She knew from Reinhold that there were frequent identity checks there. The air raid warden was pedantic and officious. The suspicion aroused by a foreign woman with a child was already enough to endanger them; and as the progress of the war became ever more threatening to loyal citizens of the Reich, so they grew ever swifter at sniffing out Jews in hiding and ever more eager to hunt them down. So above ground they stay, trembling and hoping that the bombs will spare the Werkstättenhof.

Thus things continued, until 5 November 1944, when Reinhold was away climbing or hiking in the mountains. Around midday, they heard the rising and falling wail of the sirens and Regina, following some sudden intuition, said: Today we are going to the basement. It's Sunday, so maybe there won't be anybody there.

And if they are and they ask us where we've come from?

Then we just say—

She didn't get to the point of concocting an explanation because, while they were still in the stairwell, the first bombs fell. Debris from the walls and roof tiles hailed down on the courtyard, the wood tile flooring lurched as if in an earthquake, the shock wave threw them to the ground. A miracle that they were uninjured, that they did not lose each other in the cloud of dust, that they found their way into the basement blind.

Down in the vaults, there were in fact only a few people, lying or sitting; Lucia believes she saw at most half a dozen, tenants from the block of flats facing the courtyard, who were already so frightened that they barely noticed who was bursting in. At most perhaps someone yelled, Shut the door! but their voice was either swallowed by the din or died away into a groan as the floor shook and rippled at every detonation. A fissure ran across the walls, debris and ever more dust swirled into the space, the compressed air beat against their eardrums, the light flickered, weakened until the filament barely glowed and finally died amid sighs and screams. Regina had pulled Lucia into a corner by the foundation of the fire wall, curled up into a ball there with her arm slung around her child. Her prediction, which the girl did not want to believe, rang out like a litany: Now we have to die, now we have to die, now, surely, we have to die.

Fearing suffocation in the basement, the people struggled to their feet in the gloom and hurried out into the courtyard while the bombardment was still in progress. At least three bomb craters gaped open. The roof of the Werkstättenhof had vanished and the top two storeys were engulfed in flames.

A sturdy woman, who was walking around with arms bare to the shoulder in spite of the cold, announced that the main fire station up at the Gürtel was burning too and that the infirmary on Stumpergasse had been hit, so the fire brigade was never going to come today.

After a while the group scattered. Only Regina and

Lucia stayed, sat themselves on a lump of stone, waited for an hour, two hours. They were in a kind of daze and, as a result, fearless.

Amazing, how quickly Reinhold was on the scene after that heavy air raid. Most likely, he had seen it from a distance while on his mountain hike. The memory of that anxiously longed for reunion is missing. Regina patted the worst of the dust from their clothes, used her spit and Reinhold's handkerchief to wipe the soot from her daughter's face. Before the firemen arrived, the trio had set out on the long march towards Hütteldorf among throngs of people who had been made homeless like them and were now seeking emergency lodgings with friends or relatives. Their objective was the garden house at Wolfersberg. They reached it in darkness; light flurries of snow were falling and the temperature was touching zero. From the high ground, Lucia could look out over the city. The sea of flames lifted her spirits; she felt like Nero watching Rome burn.

The following morning, or the one after it, they returned to the Werkstättenhof with Reinhold. In the passageway on Mollardgasse people were serving hot soup to the bombed out, a wonderfully delicate soup about which Lucia waxes lyrical to this day. From the staff of the soup kitchen they learned that their building had taken nineteen direct hits. The bombs had smashed through the roof and the floor of the fifth storey but, thanks to the reinforced concrete beams and central pillars, had penetrated no further and exploded on the fourth floor. On the ground and the first three floors, the bombs had done no major damage beyond tearing out the window frames. Even the stairwells and lift shafts had withstood the force of the explosions. The fourth storey had burned down so completely, both the exterior and interior walls, that Reinhold had to orientate himself by the façade of the Trade School before he could find where his workshop had stood. They searched in the rubble and white dust into which their worldly goods had been incinerated, looking for objects that might yet be usable. Pliers, files, vices had melted into shapeless forms, pointless even to pick them up, but the hammerheads had withstood the fierce heat. One un-hoped-for find was four Jewish prayer books from the belongings of Josef Treister. Regina had secretly brought them with her into the workshop in memory of her father and hidden them in a corner. The covers and spines were burnt away, but the printed pages had come unscathed through both the firestorm and the water used to put it out.

They continued their search the following day. In the meantime, Reinhold laboured to find them somewhere else to live. They could stay at most only a few nights in his summerhouse, and even that was to take a big gamble. In the cold season the allotments were deserted, making their presence even more suspicious to anyone who saw them. The neighbours can't be trusted, Reinhold said. Their eyes are everywhere. They're just lying in wait to report strangers to the police. They were forbidden to heat the house, lest smoke from the chimney stack betray them, and couldn't cook for the same reason, had they actually had anything to cook. Regina rinsed out the clothes they were wearing in cold water; in the morning they had no choice but to pull them back on still damp.

*

Four days after losing their home, Regina and Lucia ran into a roadblock. They had got as far as Hütteldorf on the way from the Werkstättenhof to Wolfersberg, at the terminus of tramline 49, and hadn't noticed the checkpoint until it was too late to avoid it.

Run on ahead, whispered Regina. Show them your identity card and vanish!

And because Lucia stubbornly remained at her side: Just go! Go! Who knows what they'll do with me!

It was thanks to Regina's presence of mind during Sunday's air raid that they had anything to show at all. At the last moment before they left the workshop, Regina had pocketed two sets of identity papers, which she'd been keeping for emergencies. One had originally been a blank child's membership card for the Alpine Club, which Reinhold had purloined from the club-house and filled out with Lucia's name. Precautionary measure, he'd explained to them the day after. It was not a recognised identity document – it didn't even have a photo – but chances were that Lucia could get through with it: she was blonde and still half a child and could pose as an orphan of the bombing and so rely on their sympathy. Regina's was a much riskier undertaking, to sham her way through the cordon with a six- or seven-year-old work ID from a nurse at the Lainz. She looked nothing like the woman in the photo and so was hiding her hair under a headscarf, which she had pulled down onto her forehead.

Please, run. Don't wait for me. Here, take the key for the summerhouse.

But Lucia was not to be dislodged. She clung to her mother's arm until they were in the line and Regina was holding out their papers to a man in knickerbockers and a quilted jacket.

What am I supposed to do with these scraps? Where's your Employment Book? Who's this then? Are you together? Where are you heading?

Hey, you listen to me! We've been bombed out. Maybe be a little bit polite?

Regina's spirited backchat is as fictional as his harsh tone. Uncertain also, whether he was content in the circumstances with the half-truth she was dishing up to him and sullenly waved them through or whether he commanded them not to move an inch while he walked away with their identity papers over to a fat, bald-headed man who had been stuffed into a long leather overcoat like a sausage skin. Whether they watched him gesticulating and pointing in their direction and the fat man glanced over, then said something, at which the other, after a moment's hesitation, doubled back, handed them their papers without a word and invited them with a movement of his head to walk on. Made up then, imagined – in any event unattested – except for the good outcome and the shaking of their knees, so violent that both she and Regina had to sit themselves down, twenty or fifty metres beyond the barrier, on a bench or an embankment, to wait until their legs could carry them again.

The following day, they set out once more for the

city centre, on foot, because the tram tracks had not yet been repaired. They met Reinhold on Mollardgasse. He was, unusually for him, grinning from ear to ear. An acquaintance of his named Richter, manager or authorised signatory for the firm Ellinger, Fröhlich & Co., which manufactured flavourings and liqueur essences on the ground floor of the Werkstättenhof, had put a shop on Gumpendorfer Straße at Reinhold's disposal. They moved in immediately. The house next door looked like a doll's house that had been flipped open for playtime, but this building had never been hit; the large shop window wasn't even cracked. The room behind the glass frontage was empty except for a large oven and offered direct access to the basement. There was probably a separate toilet and washbasin but that, and much else, Lucia says, she cannot retrieve from her memory.

The first thing Reinhold did was get the heating going, that much is certain. He found wood in the neighbourhood, beams and floorboards from ruined houses, which he pulled out of the rubble and lugged back to the shop. No idea whether he dusted them off and chopped them up out in the street nor how he came so quickly by an axe or saw. Lucia also does not know what he did the whole time in the shop apart from feeding the fire, as the oven could not be allowed to go out. Probably he simply sat there, preventing other bombed out people from claiming the premises for themselves and deflecting SS patrols or bands of fanatical Hitler Youth, who preyed on deserters and Jews in hiding. Work was over: not only because they'd found nothing they could use at the scene of the fire, apart from the hammerheads, which he had fitted with new wooden handles, but also because there was no more thin sheet metal to be had, not even of brittle, nasty Zinkal. On top of which, there was no electricity. The water pipe must still have been intact or have been patched up; at any rate, she does not remember suffering from thirst in those last five months of war, a confused tangle of dust, noise and tumult.

Day after day in their damp, musty section of the basement, Regina and she sat on a bench with no backrest and did not move. Sometimes residents of the building groped their way into the cellar with coal buckets and candles; weak, guttering light came through the batten door. They watched the shadows leaping on the brick vaults and listened to the people coughing, hawking, unlocking the padlocks, shovelling coal into buckets. Every two, three hours the pair of them, frozen to the marrow, scurried up into the shop to warm themselves for ten minutes, standing behind the oven so that they could not be seen from the street. Only in the evenings, after Reinhold had pulled down the roller shutters, were they allowed to stretch their legs above ground. Lucia does not know whether he managed to find mattresses and blankets or whether they slept on the floor fully dressed, wrapping themselves in rags and old bedside rugs. It is also unclear how he provided them, and indeed himself, with something to eat. He no longer had an income, unless he was able to collect outstanding debts on goods sold on consignment. He'll have had money somewhere already, Lucia thinks. It is not certain. It is only certain that he no longer left Regina and her alone. He didn't return to his flat in the evenings, didn't go mountaineering at the weekends. He only left the shop to gather wood or search for food. Later, when people began to loot warehouses, storage depots and freight wagons, he got his hands on a wheel of cheese so heavy he had to roll it home.

Lucia thinks it likely that Fritz Hildebrandt visited her mother on Gumpendorfer Straße as well. Perhaps, who knows, he was finally of some use and brought them bread, Sanostol or soap.

She herself no longer wanted to go outside. The droning, crashing and wailing never stopped, people scrabbled in the filth, black smoke rose. Vienna had been declared a combat zone; posters advised women with children to abandon the city. Nevertheless, we may think that Lucia from time to time took a few steps outside; how else could she claim to have seen the bills announcing executions in black letters on red? 'Being condemned by the People's Court for preparations for high treason and forfeiting permanently their rights as a citizen…' One name was familiar to her; it belonged to a worker from Leopoldstadt who, along with his wife, had been part of Regina's circle of friends. Communists, both of them. The husband wasn't executed until the beginning of 45. But Lucia must have read the relevant proclamation much earlier, on one of her excursions with Reinhold or on that evening when they discussed the turning point of the war in front of the house on Albertgasse, because in the last year of Nazi rule executions were no longer announced publicly – for lack of paper.

Lucia knows for certain that this news robbed her of speech. Mute, she sits next to her mother on the bench in the cellar. Mute, she huddles behind the oven. Mute, she turns aside. Mute, she holds her head in her hands. Questioned, she does not react.

I simply stopped speaking. I had absolutely no awareness I was doing it. My mother remarked on it afterwards, when the worst was over: Fancy! Now you're talking again!

For days on end, they could hear the din of battle. Every time a shell struck nearby the glass of the shop window shook. Then, by degrees, it grew quiet. Isolated gunshots rang out at ever greater intervals, until they heard a faint, gently swelling rasping and clattering, whose source they could not fathom even once they knew it signified salvation. Reinhold walked to the shop door, opened it and stepped down onto the pavement. Regina and Lucia followed him, remained standing on the threshold, watching over his shoulder. They saw soldiers coming up the street, purposeful and yet leisurely; some were pulling small carts of portable artillery or ammunition boxes behind them.

We'd seen the German army marching when they invaded: precision movements, tight, erect. The crack of boot on paving. But the Russians didn't march, they walked. Strolled! That was what struck me most. They had soft felt boots on and wore fur caps instead of steel helmets.

At the sight of them, Lucia's eyes started with tears. The fear was gone in an instant, she says.

This happened on an overcast April day in the year 1945, probably between two and two-thirty in the afternoon. None of them ever wanted to forget it.

*

They stayed together for a week. By then, the situation had normalised to the point that they could set about organising their life of freedom. The bodies had been gathered up and crudely buried in parks and bomb craters; the main streets had been made passable. Regina's first trip led her to a school building on Albertgasse, which now housed a field office of the Soviet military command. With her knowledge of Polish, she could have communicated tolerably in Russian. But the captain or major into whose presence she was admitted enquired about her concerns in almost faultless, Yiddish-tinged German. Then he listened to the story of survival she offered by way of explanation.

Where's the flat the fascists drove you out of? he said.

In Alsergrund, not far from the Danube Canal.

Go there and throw those people out. I'll give you one of my men to go with you. He'll see to it that you can move in today.

The building at 29 Berggasse was undamaged. Regina crossed the inner courtyard beside the Russian soldier and climbed up to the fourth storey of the rear building. The door of the flat looked exactly as it had four or five years ago, except the name plate had been replaced.

After they knocked a second time, footsteps could be heard, then the key was turned, the door was opened a crack and straightaway pulled shut.

Otkroitye! shouted the soldier and pulled his pistol. Immediately the door sprang open as if of its own accord.

On the other side of the threshold stood the wife of the couple from before, gaping in terror at the soldier, then Regina. On both sides there was recognition. Beforehand, Regina had vowed to herself that she would not give in, no matter the circumstances. But when her gaze fell on the little girl who was clutching the hem of the woman's skirt, it was clear to her that she would relinquish her claim.

The girl. She was 'mongoloid'. I couldn't put her out on the streets with her parents. I turned around and walked away. The Russian chased after me, I didn't have to explain anything to him.

What happened after that? said Reinhold, as we were sitting together in the shop on Gumpendorfer Straße for the last time.

We went back to the commander's office. I told the officer why I had given up the flat. At that he sent us back out there; we should ask around, whether there was an empty flat nearby.

To each concierge they posed the same question: which of these is a Nazi flat? Just one block further on, on the other side of the street, they struck gold. The former owners, a tax adviser and his wife, had made off to Salzburg at the end of February or beginning of March. The flat was spacious and fully furnished. Bed linen lay in the bedroom cupboard and, in their haste, the couple had left behind books, pictures and even an assortment of papers, from which emerged their complicity in the crimes of the Nazi regime.

All good? asked the soldier.

Regina nodded, put the key in the lock and had the Military Command confirm in writing that she had taken over the flat legally. That very evening she and Lucia slept on real feather beds. It was an unaccustomed experience to which they rapidly grew accustomed.

Getting new identity papers went smoothly too. Given that all their official documents had been burned in the workshop, Regina was afraid the authorities would not recognise her and Lucia's identities without protracted investigation. But when they paid a visit to the town hall, it turned out that copies of their certificates of nationality, birth and proof of residency had survived the Nazi regime and the chaos of war unscathed.

Her third mission, however, was not a success. There

are no vacancies, Regina was told, when she tried to argue her claim to be reinstated at the Lainz Hospital. She went from the head of personnel to the director of the institute, who merely shrugged his shoulders, and then back to the town hall, where she laid out the grounds and circumstances of her dismissal and pointed out the wretched views of her replacement. Her protest was in vain.

It took months, if not years, says Lucia, for my mother to win her case and be allowed to resume her duties. Because no one was willing to fire the chemist Regina herself had trained, the laboratory was split in two, so she had to work next door to this Nazi woman. What we lived off in the meantime, I don't know. Probably the money Fritz had earned. She married him in 1946. He moved in with us straight after.

The new school year had already begun in June 1945. Immediately, Lucia's passion for learning was awoken. Every morning, noisily eager for her classes, she skipped her way to school and was always the first to volunteer to wipe the blackboard because this task seemed to her the essence of a proper lesson like those she had yearned for when in hiding. Her spelling was weak, but the best girl in the class helped her with it, secretly correcting Lucia's essays under the desk. Regina found her a tutor for English and maths, on top of which she was already getting up at five o'clock every weekday to catch up on the topics from the years she had missed. Her desire to become a doctor had been firm for a long time; she won through against the wishes of her mother, who would have preferred Lucia to study chemistry like her.

A few days after the liberation, while the thunder of war could still be heard in the distance, Lucia set out for Engerthstraße in hope of a reunion, but all she could find out was that her grandmother had died at the beginning of the year. Aunt Leopoldine had turned into a haggard war widow who, at one meeting with Regina, complained that she had been classified as tainted by National Socialism and lost her work as a result. Hard to say whether Regina found the patience to listen to her or else stood up in the middle of a sentence and walked out without saying goodbye. A little later the news arrived from France that, at the beginning of March 1943, Arnold Treister had been deported to the east from the transit camp at Drancy; unknown to this day whether he perished in Sobibór or Majdanek. His wife and daughter had managed to flee from Paris to southern France where they were interned in a camp. A year after the end of the war, both returned to Vienna. Regina took them in until she was able to obtain a small flat for them on Josefstädter Straße. Her other brother, Julian, had survived the years of German occupation together with his family. He never returned to Vienna.

Eventually a letter reached them from Australia. Rudi Kraus expressed his joy that his worst fears had not been realised and regretted his forced powerlessness. 'If only I could have helped you somehow!' He was by then working as a maths teacher in a small town called Castlemaine in the heart of gold-prospecting country, and all in all he was doing well. One piece of luck was that Piroska and he had found each other again. She had managed to get out of Shanghai and battle her way to Australia; they were living together now and she had instructed him to pass on her heartfelt regards. Neither she nor he could imagine returning to Europe. If Regina was considering emigrating, she could count on their support at any time. Most of all, it was his dearest wish to take in Lucia. Until such a time, she should study her English diligently to avoid difficulties settling in.

For the moment, however, this was not an option. Both of them, mother as much as daughter, could not imagine being separated – even if Fritz Hildebrandt was once again claiming a substantial portion of Regina's time and devotion. On top of which there was Reinhold. Their bond with him remained strong; he had set up a new workshop after the war and received assurances that he could move back into the Werkstättenhof once the war damage was cleared. His ex-girlfriend Mina Gottlieb made contact with him from another corner of Australia. She implied that she would be keen to live back in Vienna with Reinhold. He vehemently dissuaded her. The people here are starving and have no way of heating themselves, he wrote. The economy is on its knees, the political situation is a mess, professionally he'd lived through better times – besides which they would surely have grown apart in their long period of separation.

If people love each other, all that is beside the point, said Regina. The problem is, you're scared stiff of committing yourself for the long term.

For eternity, he muttered.

Things weren't going as badly for Reinhold as he had suggested in his letter to Mina Gottlieb. He had a living at least and, because his material needs were modest, he could continue to pursue his passions. In the cold months of the year, he was often to be found on Heumarkt, on the ice rink, where people danced the tango and waltzes to music from a loudspeaker every Sunday from eleven. Reinhold was much in demand as a partner, Lucia says. All my girlfriends knew him.

In the second or third winter after the liberation, he

took Lucia on a skiing trip on the Dachstein. Of the hours of ascent through deep snow, she remembers the chocolate that he produced at each rest stop and administered to her in small pieces and her astonishment that, in her exhaustion, she had fallen asleep standing up. Another time, in the summer holidays, he wanted to teach her – in his calm, persevering fashion – to climb. On the premises of a climbing school in Mödling, she had to haul herself up a rock face then walk along a narrow ridge with steep drops to left and right.

It was a horribly hot day, and I was already shaking at the prospect of the descent. It was not until we were at the top that I saw you could comfortably reach the summit by a winding path on the other side. That hit me so hard I never wanted to climb again. Why all this trouble with rope, harness and spikes if you can do it another way?

Soon after this failed attempt to enthuse Lucia about mountaineering, it became apparent that Reinhold had entered into a romantic relationship. He had kept quiet about it until this point, but now the woman was pregnant and wanted to get married and, in his quandary, Reinhold sought Regina's advice.

My girlfriend, this Nelly, she comes from Rheinland. She moved to Vienna for the music. I met her at the

Alpine Club. We went dancing a few times, went on outings together, then it just happened.

So do you love her?

I do, but I'm not as young as I was, and I don't know if I'm suited to marriage, still less being a father.

It's worth trying, said Regina. You can always get divorced later. But you mustn't leave another woman in the lurch.

He knew she wasn't only referring to the shameless way he'd disowned Mina Gottlieb. Even before his relationship with Mina, while he was studying at the School of Arts and Crafts, he had been with a cheerful girl from Nuremberg – an up-and-coming ceramicist – who had likewise got pregnant. He had refused to marry her and claimed there was no proof he was the father. At this, the young woman travelled back to Germany to her parents who she hoped would support her. No one from the circle that used to meet on Pappenheimgasse ever heard from her again.

Reinhold was silent. It could be that you're right, he said finally. I'll think things over.

It is not known whether Regina was present at the marriage ceremony. Likely not, as otherwise Lucia would have gone with her. She didn't think much about it: that Reinhold, whom she had only ever been able to see as a bachelor, had suddenly become a husband and, six months later, the father of a family. His wife was pretty, neat and tastefully dressed. You could tell she came from a middle-class family. For a while, she gave the girl piano lessons, then no longer, because Lucia was bored practising the same pieces over and over and soon gave up playing the piano altogether.

It's peculiar, says Lucia. Though we met so often over the years and undoubtedly Nelly was there with us, I always just see Reinhold in front of me, alone, without his wife and without his daughter. I was so focussed on him that I didn't really notice them.

At the same time, Regina, unbroken in her curiosity about people who were different from the run of the population, opened up their flat on Albertgasse to their few remaining friends and many new ones, Reinhold's family among them. She fed them not semolina but slices of bread and butter and the debates rarely turned to politics, as if the crimes of the Nazis had rendered any thought of revolution superfluous. The dangers and failures of bygone years also rarely came up. Once, it's true, Reinhold recounted what one of his climbing comrades – a man who had been a precinct inspector or Gestapo underling between 1938 and 1945 – had recently revealed to him:

Duschka, you know, in the war I got an anonymous report. Said you were hiding two alien workers at your place.

And? said Reinhold.

I tore up the note and threw it in the wastepaper basket.

No further questions from Reinhold. Even Regina had no interest in learning more. Speculation, to this day, who had uncovered their secret, when and where.

*

Lucia was seventeen when she fell passionately in love for the first and only time, with her future husband Alfred Heilman, twenty-six. For Alfred, this was not his first love. His third or fourth had been with a Soviet foundry director's wife, at whose behest he had been awarded a place to study at the Technical University in Sverdlovsk. That city in the Urals was only one stop in a chaotic sequence – comprising persecution, flight, fighting at the front, hard labour, search for his siblings and, again, flight – which had begun in Lviv and came to a temporary stop in Vienna. He had come here to pursue his emigration to South America, sought out his last employer's cousin and then revised his plans for the future when he met her daughter – because Lucia had decided, in the meantime, to take up her father's offer. So the new life plan proposed that Alfred should continue his technical studies in Vienna and follow her to Australia afterwards. Lucia did not receive her entry visa until she was already in her second term studying medicine. Unforgotten, the four-week passage on an emigrant ship carrying a thousand passengers; unforgotten, too, the reunion on Melbourne harbour with her father, whom she had not seen for ten years and recognised at first sight. For hours, she had to describe to him every detail of their years in hiding. Possible that he only then understood to its full extent the daring of Reinhold's act of friendship.

Lucia wished herself away from Vienna because it had become more and more exhausting to have to live among former Nazis and Nazi fellow travellers. She thought that every passer-by more than a few years older than her could either have murdered Jews or willingly accepted their murder. In Castlemaine, she was freed from this idea. She had her own room in the small house with a garden where Rudi and Piroska lived. In another room, her father had set up a lab in which he conducted research into the crystalline structure of metals. But even as he worked so hard to make her feel at home in Australia, Lucia could not ward off the feeling that she had landed in the wrong place. Her problem was partly the unexpectedly strict requirements for studying medicine. She would have to apply for a place at a residential college – the cost of which, on top of the high tuition fees, far exceeded her father's financial means – and Lucia did not want to give up her studies no matter what. But that aside, she could not reconcile the population's innocence and complacency with what she had experienced.

This Castlemaine felt to me like some dreadfully sleepy backwater. The locals' chief topic of conversation was the weather, which they could talk about for hours. There were no concerts, no repertory theatre, no art cinema, no existential anxieties, not a spark of character. Simply nothing! Early in the morning, people put money out on the doorstep, the milkman brought the milk and left behind the change. No one had the idea to steal it. One year, there was not a single murder in the entire state, not one revolution in a century. It was all so virtuous. And so I wanted to go back to Vienna. When I'd made up my mind, my father showed me more of Australia. It was interesting enough. The gold prospectors were good. But there was nothing there for me. There was no old palace like on the Ringstraße, no grand civic buildings. Nothing but cottages with gardens, stood between other cottages with gardens.

The Jewish Joint Distribution Committee had covered the cost of her journey out; to finance her return, Rudi Kraus had to take out a loan, something that grieved him less than his suspicion that he would never see his daughter again. Up until his death in the mid-1980s, many letters went back and forth between Castlemaine and Vienna, and Lucia supplied him with reference books on his specialist subject. He never attempted to publish the results of his research. At some point he took in his sister, out of pity, because she was lonely in Vienna. Unknown, whether he attempted to repay the man who had once been his best friend. Not that I know of, says Lucia. Besides, there are good grounds to imagine that Reinhold would have declined any form of compensation for something he had done with a pure heart.

Lucia and Alfred married soon after her return. By then, he had had to give up his technical studies because it took all his time to make money for accommodation and food. He had arrived in Vienna with two dollars and one pair of tattered shoes and had launched his career bartering and trading currencies on the black market in front of the former Rothschild Hospital. After that he opened, in turn and with various partners and increasing rates of profit: a coffee roastery, a grocer's, Vienna's first supermarket. He worked hard and was seldom at home. Lucia is convinced, nevertheless, that they had a fulfilling marriage. Her first daughter, Viola, entered the world in 1955; her second, Monika, in 1968. In between came the birth of a boy who died at four months from a serious heart defect. His death plunged Lucia into a deep depression from which she did not escape until they took a cruise down the Danube and on to the Crimea. After graduating late as a doctor and following internships in several hospitals, she worked as ward physician in the urology department at the Barmherzigen Brüder (Brothers of Charity), then as a school doctor in the same gymnasium where she had once furnished Grimm's fairy tale 'The Wishing Table' with a self-assured, prescient title. Everyone has to know how to help themselves.

Let these be two images of placid retirement at different times: in the first, Regina, in her old age, sits in Café Hummel every afternoon and, like a benevolent spider, waits for another visitor to the coffee house to become entangled in her fine-spun web of curiosity and compassion. It's never long before a stranger is keeping her company. They've barely sat down and Regina has already got them talking; in half to three-quarters of an hour, she has learned how they live, their grievances, what they long for.

The second scene is at the family's small holiday home in Semmering, where Lucia and Alfred have fled the heat of the big city. Lucia devotes herself to her hobby, embroidering pictures, sticking to the pattern as strictly as she once did with her crafting in Reinhold's workshop. Alfred sits next to her and pulls a thread through the canvas with a calm, sure hand. He is responsible for the single-coloured background; she wants to make the motif, a bouquet in a vase, glow in many varied hues. Perhaps they chat about their daughters, their two lively grandchildren, the journeys that Lucia longs to make and for which Alfred can find no enthusiasm because as a young man he wandered so far across the earth against his will. After a while, the conversation arrives at Lucia's departed mother, to whom they owe their own union, and at her baffling dependence on Fritz Hildebrandt, who managed, while Regina was still in the nursing home, to betray her with another woman.

Really unbelievable what people will do to one another, says Alfred, then lays down his needle and lights up a cigarette.

Men! says Lucia. Then she thinks of Reinhold and she finds her verdict too hasty.

*

No, he doesn't want to do it. They should put it out of their minds. When he's retired, they can discuss it again.

In the mid-1960s, Lucia learned that the memorial complex of Yad Vashem was paying tribute to those who had risked their own lives to save Jews. From then on, she was determined to put Reinhold forward for the honour. He baulked at the suggestion not only, she believes, because he found celebrations abhorrent on principle but also because he was afraid of losing customers. Who knows whether buyers might not have vanished as a result and climbing friends shunned him in the Alpine Club? He gave up his workshop at seventy-nine years old, had undertaken his last climbing tour long before that. But it was not until he was ninety that he dropped his objections to Lucia's proposal. From then, it took barely a year before Reinhold was honoured as Righteous Among the Nations in the presence of his family and the Heilmans, several ambassadors and a minister. Yet for Lucia, this was not enough.

It doesn't count. My elder daughter took care of the submission to Yad Vashem. She has perfect English, which speeds things up. She arranged everything. I only really did anything when I read the appeal from Steven Spielberg in the Jewish community's newspaper. For Holocaust survivors to make themselves available for video interviews. I got in touch immediately.

But the preservation of her life story in the archive of the Shoah Foundation didn't satisfy her either. She went into more and more schools to tell young people about her experiences. Reinhold Duschka as a model for the coming generation: this was her drive and her aim. Because, as she says, there are heaps of books about the victims, about the perpetrators as well, no question – but hardly any about the rescuers. People know Oskar Schindler, with luck Anton Schmid and three or four others. If any at all. So Lucia didn't hesitate for a second when she was invited to take part in a theatre project, *The Last Witnesses*, which premiered at the Vienna Burgtheater in October 2013 – half a year after a plaque to Reinhold's memory had been fixed to the façade of the Werkstättenhof. The director Matthias Hartmann staged the piece; the writer Doron Rabinovici selected the six Jewish survivors of the Nazi terror. (The seventh person chosen, the Romany woman Ceija Stojka, had died at the beginning of the year.) While young actors read out their memories, the six sat behind a synthetic scrim which, as the projection screen for all kinds of photos and documents, both made their forms visible and obscured them at the same time, an aesthetic device of deliberate symbolic power and with the inadvertent side effect that the elderly women and men had to fight to stay awake as the heat from the spotlights built up behind the screen. Towards the end of the performance, they were led out by the actors, one by one, onto the forestage, from where they could deliver a personal message to the public.

The performances – on stages in Salzburg, Berlin, Hamburg and other cities as well as at the Burgtheater – were sold out; the audiences were shaken. Many of them remained in the theatre long after the final applause because they wanted to take part in the discussions organised with these witnesses to history. It was in this way, after the premiere in Vienna, that Lucia met Leo Graf, who had worked for Reinhold Duschka for almost eight years, from October 1952 to August 1960. Both were compelled to swap stories about him. Reinhold's daughter Hellgard Janous joined them at some of their meetings. From the very first it was clear to them how little, ultimately, they knew about him.

*

For example, Leo Graf, born 1927 and raised in Vienna. His parents separated when he was still a child. His father was a Nazi, his mother listened secretly to Radio London and spread the news as rumours around their block. When he was fifteen, Leo was conscripted from the school bench to be a Luftwaffe auxiliary and from there was seamlessly adopted, as he puts it, into the German armed forces. Whenever he was given home leave, he was drawn to the mountains, where he felt delivered from obedience and subjection. He ended up a prisoner of the Americans and returned to the city of his birth at the beginning of 1946. There he began to study chemistry but had to break off his studies after both of his parents died within a month. At the suggestion of a friend, he did an abbreviated apprenticeship for war veterans as a tinsmith. After his journeyman's examination, he switched to a building firm, which didn't treat him badly. And so he might have continued, forty years until retirement.

But then he met Reinhold Duschka in the Edelweiß section of the Austrian Alpine Club. They went on expeditions together. Their first was by ski into the Stubai Alps where Reinhold showed him how an instructor should lead beginners. Save the strong from overestimating their strength; make the energy of the weakest your yardstick. Advice that made sense to him. By the following summer, they were leading a group of fifteen mountaineers from Col du Midi over Mont Blanc, and Leo was deeply impressed by the serenity of the older man, who either passed over impertinent remarks without a word or courteously deflected them. I'm sure, he says, in a situation like that, I'd have insisted on my authority. He mentions an incident that was laughingly circulated around their section's clubhouse, in which one participant on a training course had accidentally stepped on Reinhold's head with crampons strapped to his boots and thus elicited – only after some delay – the lapidary request that he should climb back down when a suitable opportunity arose.

It may be that Leo recognised himself in Reinhold. This was true for the externals like thin hair and lean frame, extended to their indifference to fashion, consumption and luxury, and also manifested itself in the fact that they met their wives in the Alpine Club. Neither used big words. Both were reliable. That's why climbing in a rope team meant so much to them, because it demanded trust and responsibility. And yet, like all inveterate mountaineers, they were half egotist, half autistic in their private lives. Hard for their relatives to cope with.

One day, Reinhold said: I've heard you're a trained tinsmith. Can you handle metal?

Yes. Zinc and iron sheet.

Then you have the skills to work with brass and copper as well.

Of course. And if not, you'll teach me.

On the first day of the following month, he began working for Reinhold in his studio. He did not for a moment regret it, because Reinhold was a thoughtful master who never made a show of his superiority. Besides which, Leo considered himself lucky to be involved in the entire production process from the unworked sheet metal to the finished, hand-crafted article. That was an experience he'd have had to forego as a tinsmith. And third, they still had enough time to go skiing and mountain climbing. They worked flat out through the autumn, often overtime and with a temporary assistant who looked after Reinhold's showroom on Floriani-gasse, in order to keep up with their orders. Sometimes even their families had to step in: Nelly at the shop, Leo's wife and his daughter Elfie at home on the kitchen table, wrapping reed grass around teapot handles.

Once the Christmas season was over, they shut up the workshop and went skiing for two weeks. The summers were free as well because Reinhold had no desire to

—

produce for stock when there was no way of predicting which items would be particularly in demand come high season. They undertook strenuous tours, not only in Austria but also in the French and Swiss Alps. But they rarely did so together. Each of us had his own partners, says Leo. The age gap alone saw to that. Most of the time I went with people my own age.

So it went, year after year, with a steady stream of orders and an instinctive mutual understanding. In the end, it was happenstance that induced Leo to quit his job with Reinhold. The pay was modest and, because he knew that his boss barely earned more than he did, it never occurred to him to ask for a pay rise. One day he read in a leaflet that the post office was looking for staff; he contacted them and was taken on. A good place to work, back then, with regular pay increments and a secure pension. But his years with three months of holiday, split between summer, winter and Easter, were over. Mostly he only met Reinhold at the Edelweiß section clubhouse on Walfischgasse. Their last big group tour has stayed in his memory – 1959 it must have been, because Reinhold was just shy of sixty, Leo a little over thirty – along the southwest ridge of the Schreckhorn in the Bernese Alps, a four-thousander, reckoned by mountaineers to be especially difficult.

I almost dissolved with admiration. I thought to myself: I want to still be able to do that when I'm as old as him. And thirty years later, I did do it.

Leo first learned that Reinhold had concealed a Jewish woman and her daughter in his workshop for four years when it was reported in the newspaper that he had been honoured as Righteous Among the Nations. I was flabbergasted, he says. Reinhold had never spoken of it, not even hinted. They had spoken little with each other in any case, still less about anything not to do with their work or with mountaineering. Not a word of politics. No gossip. Nothing about childhood, family home, the war, resistance. Unmentioned also were the yearning for closeness and the necessity of changing the world.

That was down to me as well. If I hear something of interest, I'm all ears. But questioning someone? I wouldn't think of it, still wouldn't. And Reinhold never told you anything off his own bat. When I read the article in the newspaper, my admiration for him grew immeasurably. Though, when I think about it now, it doesn't surprise me. I would have expected it of him.

Reinhold Duschka died in May 1993, a month before his ninety-third birthday, being as he was half a year younger than his century. Leo Graf composed the only really personal obituary, for the newsletter of the Edelweiß section, whose members presumably only then learned the truth about the man they had viewed – wistfully or with mild amusement – as a relic of a lost age of Alpinism. 'For you, it was natural and simply not worth mentioning that in a time of inhumanity you lived up to your ideals as a human being. And for that, in this moment when history threatens to repeat itself, I would like particularly to thank you.'

*

Hellgard Janous also did not know for a long time that her father had saved two people. She found out by chance, soon after he had informed her, Frau Steinig is not at all well, we absolutely have to visit her, do you have time next weekend? During their visit to the hospital, Hellgard witnessed a conversation between Regina and Reinhold that revealed their shared history to her. That was in the mid-1970s when she was past twenty-five years old, and it changed the image she had had of her father until that moment: a taciturn loner who came out of his shell only in the company of other mountaineers or younger women and who, for as long as she could remember, had never really been there.

Either he was at work, she says, or he was climbing.

At those times, wife and daughter sat at home, hoping he had not had an accident. Three times, he had: on Peilstein, Schneeberg and the Rax. The first fall passed off relatively lightly: he fell onto the rope and bruised a few ribs. On the second occasion, his companion slipped and fell over a cliff edge into the abyss. Reinhold tried to hold onto the rope, which was unspooling itself at a frantic pace. By the time he'd succeeded in stopping the fall, he'd burned the palms of both his hands. The wounds began to suppurate and he got blood poisoning. The worst was his fall on the Rax: he broke both jawbones and knocked out a number of teeth. His upper lip had to be stitched up several times. An ugly scar remained, on account of which he grew a moustache.

His wife was not only a piano teacher; she also performed for many years as a choral singer in the Vienna Singverein. In spite of the demands of her concerts, tours and recording sessions, he left the care of Hellgard to her. If she had to, she took the child with her to the final rehearsal at the Musikverein; on one occasion Hellgard had to accompany her to the Salzburg Festival. Only when Nelly was out of town did he take Hellgard to school in the mornings. In the evenings, after her lessons and after-school club, she did not see him again until he returned from his workshop. He took no interest in her school day. He went neither to parents' evenings nor to her teachers' consultation hours. Admittedly, he didn't scold her either, says Hellgard, if she came home far too late or with a bad mark.

The patience he had mustered for Lucia remained hidden from his daughter. He was hot-headed and irascible when he had to help her with her maths – this was later, when she was at the gymnasium – and she did not immediately grasp his explanations. Or when he could not find a shirt in the wardrobe. Or when he had mislaid his bunch of keys and blamed Nelly for it. Whereas outside the house or in a genuinely dangerous situation, he was calm incarnate. He seems to have struggled to tolerate in his family what he had granted to Regina and Lucia: that they had a right to space in his life. But it never came to open conflict. Nelly and Hellgard learned ice dancing, went skiing, accepted that on their excursions he preferred other people around him. They would have had no chance of keeping up with him on his ski tours and mountain climbs, and they couldn't get excited by the prospect either. During the annual winter holiday in Tyrol, they were left to their own devices, since Reinhold spent his days on strenuous ski tours and went to sleep early in the evenings. If my mother hadn't allowed him the freedom to go his own way, says Hellgard, the marriage would have undoubtedly fallen apart. In return, Reinhold agreed to visit Nelly's relatives in Krefeld and Cologne over the Christmas holidays, even though some of them considered themselves rather superior and made sure their brother- or son-in-law felt it too.

Once he was too old to go mountaineering, they would set off at the beginning of July each year on an extended holiday. For six weeks it was them and the Volkswagen, cautiously but safely driven by Reinhold, journeying through Corsica, Morocco, half of Europe. Hellgard didn't get to see much though. Like her mother, she was obliged to adapt herself to his ways. Pitching tents, pumping up airbeds, going swimming, looking around buildings – but only from the outside; he had no interest in museums and never took time to rest. Then back to the long hours – half days – that Nelly and she occupied by going on walks or playing badminton while their father explored dunes, cliffs or gorges with their travelling companions, two unattached women from his circle of acquaintance. Hellgard's birthday, which fell during their time away, was not much celebrated: a bar of chocolate was her usual gift. That on one occasion they went out for a meal was the height of emotion.

Reinhold's origins, his childhood. Because he never talked about it, says Hellgard, I never asked him. She does not know who his parents were, when and how they lived and earned their living, whether in the rear courtyard of a tenement building, in a flat, a worker's house, in a garden colony. Were there books on their shelves? Did pictures hang on their walls? What kind? Was there a dog, a cat, a pair of budgies, a rabbit hutch behind the house, a dovecote under the roof? Where did he go to school, what was the name of his favourite teacher, who did he fight on his way home and who came to his defence in a fight? How did he do on his apprenticeship, under which master? Was he an only child or did he have siblings? If yes, how many? What was in store for them? Where were they laid to rest? Incinerated, trapped under rubble or hastily buried? On which field of honour?

Hellgard believes she remembers a black-bordered envelope lying open one day on the bureau, news that an elderly woman had departed this life. Perhaps that was about his sister; she cannot swear to it. At any rate, he didn't go to the funeral, nor did he ever indicate a desire or intention to revisit the city of his birth. On another occasion, when Hellgard was nineteen, he was expecting a female visitor, who had phoned to say she was coming, and was, exceptionally for him, in rather a flap about it. Here now was the daughter from the relationship with the pleasure-loving woman from Nuremberg – or not. As before, Reinhold had his doubts.

It's certain that he was neither baptized nor devout. That he didn't smoke and took care to eat healthily but was not averse to a glass of wine in his later years, when he indulged himself more than he used to. That he played Skat with his son-in-law and taught chess, draughts and twenty-one to his grandchildren. That he sometimes told Count Bobby jokes. That he never lost his German accent. That he put on a Berlin accent for fun. That he worshipped Josef Hoffmann, rhapsodized about Karl Kraus, quoted from Goethe, Gerhart Hauptmann, Wilhelm Busch. That he possessed a library of a couple of thousand volumes. That he read the newspaper – and later, when they had a television set, watched the news – every day.

In spite of that, I never had the feeling he cared about politics. It wasn't even clear to me that he was against the Nazis. He just never expressed an opinion on it. I don't think he ever even went to vote, not once. Somehow his political years were behind him.

By contrast, Gerald, Hellgard's elder son, saw his

grandfather as a politically aware man. One who sympathised with the occupiers of the Hainburger Au, the protesters who prevented the Danube wetlands being destroyed for a proposed hydro-electric power station. A man who revered the Green politician Freda Meissner-Blau and took pleasure in reading the newspaper columns of the depth psychologist Erwin Ringel, in which he did battle with the collective neuroses of his fellow Austrians.

Gerald was three when he was handed over to his grandparents for a few days for the birth of his brother. From this time stems the deep closeness between grandson and grandfather, which was to last until the latter's death eighteen years later. Not that the boy got on badly with his grandmother; he liked her for her artistic flair and for the interesting people around her. And yet Nelly was fond of platitudes and convention, including in her dealings with children, whereas Reinhold never imposed absurd restrictions or rules on him, in keeping with his life philosophy: to constrain no one nor allow himself to be constrained.

My grandfather was a great lover of freedom and he made use of his freedom, even if his family suffered as a result. Aside from that, he had an amazingly kind, warm way of dealing with people, which appealed to children and women especially. With men it was more his sporting prowess that impressed them.

Gerald learned a thing or two from Reinhold – and not only how to chop wood, grip well when climbing, or cut a bracelet from a sheet of copper. The stories that Reinhold told about his life, about his mistakes and his failures, these too left a lasting impression on the boy. Only occasionally did he wonder if his grandpa really made these mistakes or just invented them in order to make him understand something, such as in the story of his supposed passion for war: that Reinhold had been so vociferously gung-ho as a seventeen year old that he wanted to go to war of his own free will. Sheer luck that at the army medical he was declared unfit to serve on grounds of myopia and poor blood vessels. Otherwise, he claimed, he would have had to join in with the entire madness and would have bought it in the end too.

I was never so stupid again after that.

But in other respects, he could still be stupid: something he only realised when he nearly fulfilled his secret desire for a pretty, young female fellow climber. They had been fooling around in a hut or during a rest at the summit, Reinhold said, getting closer and closer to each other until eventually she said to him: You have one free wish from me. What do you want? Without thinking, he wished for a kiss and got it. A person could fall head-over-heels in love with you, she said to him afterwards. But it would never work between us in the long term: the age difference is just too big.

More out of politeness than interest, Gerald asked: Did something still happen between you after that?

Absolutely not. If as a young man you're too stupid or timid to show a woman that you like her, you pay the price. As an older man you have the courage, but she doesn't want you any more.

Gerald never doubted for a second that the most exciting story Reinhold had lived through was true. Unlike his mother, he had grown up knowing how Lucia had been saved. There had been for him no moment of abrupt discovery and, even if there had been, it would not have surprised him. As Gerald sees it, Reinhold might almost have been created for intelligent resistance. Because, in the first place, as a climber he was used to depending on another person and being responsible for another person. And, secondly, because he had those personal qualities that helped keep the risks as low as possible: self-discipline, discretion, independence, understanding of human beings.

My grandfather knew what he could ask of someone. He wasn't vain, that was another advantage. He acted according to his convictions, but he avoided open confrontation, so his enemies couldn't land a punch on him. He didn't sacrifice himself. He valued his own life as highly as another person's. That's why, for me, he's an example.

And these are snapshots from the life of an exemplary grandfather:

Reinhold in his favourite spot: a cosy, grey wing-back chair.

Reinhold having his breakfast, which consisted of a Graham bread roll with cottage cheese, onion and the juice of a clove of garlic.

Reinhold in the doorway. Suddenly, he stretches up his arms and starts doing pull-ups on his fingertips.

Reinhold in an apron and short trousers weeding his allotment, two hundred square metres growing sour cherries, cherries, apples, pears, gooseberries, red- and blackcurrants.

Reinhold far out to sea on a family holiday in Italy and on the beach his grandson, who every few minutes makes sure to spot the long-distance swimmer.

Reinhold and Nelly every Saturday afternoon in their comfy chairs in front of the TV. Their favourite programme flickers across the screen, the one with Heinz Conrads, the popular actor and singer of Wienerlied.

—

Reinhold on the balcony on his exercise bike, which he was still pedalling at ninety.

Reinhold in the living room, where he and the exercise bike have migrated, because passers-by had been tracking his sessions on the balcony and applauding.

Reinhold greeting neighbours and acquaintances on the street in his typical way: arms half raised, the backs of his hands waving back and forth, and laughing his bleating and yet thoroughly charming laugh.

Reinhold made this same gesture in the ceremonial hall of the Bank für Arbeit und Wirtschaft, where the Israeli ambassador presented him with a medal and certificate from Yad Vashem. After the addresses from the diplomats and politicians, he was asked up to say a few words from the podium next to which Lucia's little granddaughter was romping about. Gerald waited with bated breath. What will he say now? he thought.

Reinhold raised his arms in greeting, looked over at the girl with a smile and said: That's what pleases me most, when I see children today running around like that.

No mention of the fact that without his courage this child would not have existed. That was typical of him too, says Gerald.

Envoi

For Dr Rudolf Mader, because year after year he gave Regina a certificate for Reinhold Duschka. To tell the truth, he must have run into Regina sometimes after the Liberation, when she too was living on Albertgasse. But Lucia never heard of it, nor can she say whether her mother had any further contact with him. His nephew, the painter Heribert Mader, visited his uncle several times between 1955 and 1960, while he was a student. His flat had been damaged in the last days of the war. After it was rebuilt, Dr Mader opened a surgery in the building, where he worked until his death at the beginning of March 1966. His brother Karl, Heribert's father, had served as a major in the German armed forces in the far north before being executed as a conspirator in the aftermath of Stauffenberg's abortive assassination attempt of July 1944. Fraternal biographies in military grey, half buried in darkness, half bathed in light.

For the resistance fighter from Regina's circle of friends, whose execution was publicly proclaimed.

The identity of the slain man remains unclear. I think he was called Reimas, says Lucia. But no one among the executed Austrians has that name or anything that sounds like it, except for the five men and two women of the family Remeš, who were indeed beheaded by the regional court in Vienna but came from the Moravian village of Jankovice. None of them would have been present at the meetings in Regina's kitchen. The nearest we get to the name Lucia remembers is the communist Leopold Ram, born 1895, scaffolder by profession, resident of Leopoldstadt in Vienna, arrested 18 November 1942, condemned on 14 December 1943, beheaded on 25 February 1944. In the photos taken by the Gestapo, which make clear that he was tortured after his arrest, Lucia no longer recognises him. But this is no reason to say definitively that he was not among her mother's acquaintances. His wife, says Lucia, was raped by Soviet soldiers after the Liberation and then took her own life.

For Lucia's friend Erna Dankner from Pappenheimgasse, who was still alive when Lucia had assumed she was dead. The lorry in front of the building housing the 'collection flats', the girl falling from the bed of the lorry onto the roadway, the rear wheel that ran her over, and then her body, which offered a slight but implacable resistance to every movement. Not until seventy years later would Lucia learn that what she had seen or been told was not correct. Since it is proven that Erna, with her parents Moshe and Cipre, was deported to Auschwitz the following year, in the thirty-second transport of Austrian Jews, which departed from Vienna's Aspang station on 17 July 1942 and two days later reached its destination. Her death in the gas chamber would have been the fate of Lucia, of Regina as well. Had he not existed, Reinhold Duschka.